I walked toward the car... ach was scared. As I got closer, I looked at the license plate and repeated the number to myself, trying to remember it. A man got out of the car. It was him. He was wearing a trench coat today, and a tweed cap like longshoremen wear. But it was him.

He said, "What can I do for you, young man?"

"I was just looking at your car," I said. "It's nice."

"Thanks. Anything else?"

I kept looking at him, trying to figure him out.

"It's a '46," I said, "right?"

"It is."

"They make a coupe?" I asked. "Or a convertible?"

"I am not a car salesman," the man said.

"I was just asking," I said.

"Fine," he said. "Now you've seen it, run along."

The other Owls had stopped practice and were watching us.

"I'm not doing anything," I said.

"If you don't run along," the man said, "I'll give you reason to."

There was something in his voice, like a piece of broken glass. I nodded and turned, and walked back to the other guys:

OTHER BOOKS YOU MAY ENJOY

Robert B. Parker

EDENVILLE OWLS

PUFFIN

PUFFIN BOOKS

Published by the Penguin Group

Penguin Young Readers Group, 345 Hudson Street, New York, New York 10014, U.S.A.

Penguin Group (Canada), 90 Eglinton Avenue East, Suite 700,
Toronto, Ontario, Canada M4P 2Y3 (a division of Pearson Penguin Canada Inc.)

Penguin Books Ltd, 80 Strand, London WC2R 0RL, England

Penguin Ireland, 25 St Stephen's Green, Dublin 2, Ireland (a division of Penguin Books Ltd)

Penguin Group (Australia), 250 Camberwell Road, Camberwell, Victoria 3124, Australia
(a division of Pearson Australia Group Pty Ltd)

Penguin Books India Pvt Ltd, 11 Community Centre,
Panchsheel Park, New Delhi - 110 017, India

Penguin Group (NZ), 67 Apollo Drive, Rosedale, North Shore 0632, New Zealand
(a division of Pearson New Zealand Ltd)

Penguin Books (South Africa) (Pty) Ltd, 24 Sturdee Avenue,
Rosebank, Johannesburg 2196, South Africa

Registered Offices: Penguin Books Ltd, 80 Strand, London WC2R 0RL, England

First published in the United States of America by Philomel Books,
a division of Penguin Young Readers Group, 2007
This Sleuth edition published by Puffin Books, a division of Penguin Young Readers Group, 2008

1 3 5 7 9 10 8 6 4 2

THE LIBRARY OF CONGRESS HAS CATALOGED THE PHILOMEL BOOKS EDITION AS FOLLOWS:

Parker, Robert B., 1932–
Edenville Owls / Robert B. Parker
p. cm.
Summary: Fourteen-year-old Bobby, living in a small Massachusetts town just after World
War II, finds himself facing many new challenges as he tries to pull together his coachless
basketball team, cope with new feelings for his old friend, Joanie, and discover the identity
of the mysterious stranger who seems to be threatening his teacher.
ISBN 978-0-399-24656-2 (hardcover)
[1. Friendship—Fiction. 2. Basketball—Fiction. 3. Teachers—Fiction. 4. War—Fiction.
5. Prejudices—Fiction. 6. Coming of age—Fiction.
7. Massachusetts—History—20th century—Fiction.] I. Title.
PZ7.P2346Ede 2007 [Fic]—dc22 2006034533

Puffin Books ISBN 978-0-14-241161-2

Printed in the United States of America

Design by Katrina Damkoehler.

For Joanie Hall of Swampscott

EDENVILLE
OWLS

THE radio in our living room was about four feet tall. It was made of dark wood. It had legs and a lot of ornate carving that made me think about church. We used to sit in the living room every night and listen to it. My father would often read while we listened, but my mother and I mostly sat and looked at the radio. I sort of always wondered why we did that.

I remember we listened to stuff like One Man's Family and The Kraft Music Hall. But mostly I remember events. I was really little when we gathered around to hear about some king who was quitting to marry some woman who was American. Everybody seemed shocked, but it seemed like the right choice to me. I mean, if he loved her. . . .

All my life I listened to President Roosevelt on the radio. I remember actually thinking he was in his den, sitting by the fireplace while he had his fireside chats with us. Nearly all my life I had listened to the war news on the radio. Germany invades Poland. Japs bomb Pearl Harbor. Allies invade Normandy. Germany surrenders. Japan surrenders.

Then in April of 1945 President Roosevelt died. And in September of 1945 the war ended. So when I entered the eighth grade that fall, right after Labor Day, while the Tigers were playing the Cubs in the World Series, everything seemed to have changed.

CHAPTER 1

AT Center Junior High School we played six-man football in the fall, and regular baseball in the spring. But we had no gym, so we didn't have a basketball team until seventh grade, when my friend Russell and I decided to start one. Nick said he'd play. And Billy, and Manny. We wanted to call ourselves something kind of tough: the Tigers, or maybe the Wolverines. But when Russell and I went to New Bedford to buy the jerseys, all they had were yellow ones with a picture of an owl, so we became the Edenville Owls instead.

We hitchhiked to most games wearing our Owls uniforms under our clothes and taking turns carrying the basketball. Sometimes an adult would pick us up and give us a lecture about the dangers of hitchhiking, but no one paid any attention. It was the way we traveled. When we weren't playing we hung out together. Play pinball at Spag's Spa. Sit on the benches outside the Village Shop at the top of the wharf and listen to the jukebox through the screen door. Sometimes we fished for scup and blowfish off the dock. Blowfish weren't good to eat, but if you rubbed their stomachs they'd blow up and you could skip them across the water. We hung around together so much that people just began to call us the Owls. My mother told me no good would come of hanging out with them. But most of the kids liked us. Except the jerks.

In the eighth grade our teacher was new. Last year's teacher had been fired, everyone said, because she was a drunk. All the grown-ups told us that wasn't the case, but grown-ups tell you a lot of junk. We hoped it was true, and after a while, we kind of remembered her being drunk. This year's teacher was named Claudia Delaney. She wrote it on the blackboard the first day. Not just Miss Delaney, but the whole name, Claudia Delaney.

The Owls were sitting where we always sat, in the back seat of each of the five rows. I was in the middle between Russell and Nick. I had a copy of *Black Mask Magazine* in my lap and was reading it below the desk so Miss Delaney couldn't see it. As she stretched to write, her skirt pulled tight.

"Ming!" Russell said beside me.

I looked up. Russell nodded toward Miss Delaney.

4

"Hubba, hubba," I whispered.

Miss Delaney turned around.

"Do you five boys always sit back there?" she said.

"Yes," Nick said.

"You would be the Owls," Miss Delaney said.

"Hoot, hoot," I said.

Everyone laughed, including Miss Delaney.

Billy was always scared of teachers. And Manny was a Cape Verdean colored guy and was very careful about everything. Mostly Russell and I and Nick were the ones that talked.

"I've heard about you," Miss Delaney said.

"We're not so bad," I said.

"Oddly enough," Miss Delaney said, "that's what I heard."

Some of the girls giggled. None of us liked that too much. We wanted people to think we were pretty bad. Miss Delaney went to the board and wrote: "The boy walked to school."

"We'll start this morning," Miss Delaney said, "by reviewing some of the basic rules of grammar that you might have forgotten over the summer. What are the subject and the verb of this sentence?"

All of us groaned.

"I don't like it either," Miss Delaney said, "but we have to be able to speak the language."

I put up my hand. She nodded at me.

"We can already speak the language," I said. "How come we got to speak it a certain way?"

"Manners, mostly," she said. "Like table manners, and appearance. It's mostly about other people's impression of you."

"What if you don't care about impressing other people?" I said.

She smiled.

"It's sort of a matter of freedom," she said. "As long as you know how to speak the language, you can choose the way you want to speak it," she said. "But if you don't know correct English, you can only speak what you know."

She was different. Most teachers got annoyed with me when I asked questions like that. Sometimes I was really trying to figure it out. Sometimes I did it to annoy them. Miss Delaney didn't get annoyed. She gave me a serious answer. And she was very pretty too.

CHAPTER 2

IT was cold and raining on a Saturday morning, the first week of October, so the Owls took the bus to Eastfield for a practice game against the high school JV team. Russell had arranged the game. He was kind of bossy, and did all the arranging.

It was about a five-mile ride to Eastfield High School. We sat in the back of the bus. Edenville didn't have a high school, so we'd be going to Eastfield ourselves in a couple of years.

"Listen to this," Russell said. "You know how the state tourney decided to include JV teams?"

Nick said, "So there'll be the regular high school tournament and a JV one?"

Russell nodded.

"Well, there's a slot from each region for an independent team."

"In the JV tournament?" Billy said.

"Yeah. I guess they didn't have enough JV teams."

"And," I said, "the high school coaches like to have kids playing before they get to high school."

"Development program," Manny said.

He was a very quiet guy. Probably had to do with being a colored guy with mostly white guys. Maybe it was just how he was. But when he did say something, it was usually not a dumb thing.

"So I signed us up," Russell said.

"For the state tourney?"

"Sure," Russell said. "We win our region and we go to Boston Garden."

"Boston Garden?"

"You think we can make it to Boston Garden?" Billy said.

"You got me at center," Russell said.

"Oh boy," Billy said.

"Hey," Russell said, "you've seen my pivot shot."

Russell stood and demonstrated in the back of the bus. The bus driver saw him in the rearview mirror.

"Sit down, kid," the bus driver said.

"I guess he doesn't want to see your pivot shot either," Nick said.

Russell grinned and made a little head fake and sat down holding the basketball on his lap.

"Everybody will see it at the Garden," he said.

Russell was six foot one in the eighth grade, but he wasn't too well coordinated, and he didn't have very good hands. Still, he was taller than most kids our age. It helped him get rebounds and he scored a lot on put-backs.

The high school JVs were already doing a layup drill when we came out of the locker room. The gym smelled like floor wax and disinfectant. It had a big echo-y quality. There were stands all around the gym. No one was in the stands, but they were impressive anyway. What would it be like in Boston Garden? The Owls began to shoot around a little. We couldn't really do a layup drill with two lines even if we knew how. There weren't enough of us. There were eleven guys on the high school JVs, and they had a coach. And the high school coach himself was there too. The nervous feeling was in my stomach. The varsity captain was there with the varsity coach, and he agreed to referee. We lined up for the tip the way we always did. Russell at center. Nick and Manny at the forwards, Billy and me at guard. Billy had a pretty good set shot. And I usually brought the ball up.

The JV center got the tip even though Russell was taller. He sent it to a forward, who passed to the other forward, who passed it back for a layup. It wasn't a good start and it didn't get better. It wasn't that they were so much better players. But they knew what to do with the ball, and what to do on defense. Our plan was mostly to have me bring the ball up, see if someone was open, or try to get the ball in to Russell so he could turn around with his famous pivot shot and shoot over the guy guarding him. Except every time I did get it in to him, one of the other guys on the JVs dropped back and they double-teamed him and he lost the ball a lot.

Russell got six points. Billy got a couple of set shots. Nick drove by his man a couple times for layups. And Manny got a rebound and put it in. I got four foul shots and missed three of them. We lost forty-eight to seventeen.

The high school coach came into the locker room while we were getting dressed.

"You guys got a coach?" he said.

"No," Russell said.

"You need one," he said.

"We can't get nobody to do it," Russell said.

The coach shrugged.

"Too bad," he said. "You sure do need coaching."

It was still raining and cold while we waited for the bus across the street from the high school. The salty smell of the harbor was pretty strong. It was stronger than it was on nice days. I wondered why that was.

"We're awful," Manny said.

"Yeah," Nick said. "He's right. We need a coach."

"I asked everybody," Russell said. "Nobody's got time to coach us, that knows anything."

"We'll think of something," I said.

"Yeah?" Billy said. "Like what?"

"I don't know," I said. "I'll figure it out."

CHAPTER **3**

BILLY and I didn't do our math homework. So we had to stay after school and do it and hand it in to the office before we could leave. I was finished with mine, but Billy was still working on his and I was looking out the second-floor window waiting for him. I saw Miss Delaney come out of the side door and walk across the school yard. A tall man came around the corner of the school and walked up to her. They stopped and faced each other. He had on a trench coat and a dark snap-brimmed hat, like businessmen wore.

My God, did she have a boyfriend? I never thought about teachers having boyfriends. I mean, Miss Delaney was good-looking and all, but . . . it was embarrassing to think about.

I watched them talk. He was nodding his head and she was shaking hers. He put his hand on her shoulder. She pushed it away. He put his hand on her shoulder again. He must have had a hard hold on her the second time. She tried to twist away and couldn't. He leaned in toward her and she slapped him and he took hold of both her shoulders.

I pushed open the window.

"Hey," I yelled, "let her alone."

"What?" Billy said.

He jumped up and ran to the window.

The tall man let go of Miss Delaney and turned and stared up at us. Miss Delaney went back inside the school and shut the door. I couldn't see the guy very well because his hat was down over his eyes. And I was pretty sure he couldn't really see us from that angle. He looked down at the door where Miss Delaney had gone in, and back at the open window, and then he turned fast and went around the corner of the school.

"Holy hell," Billy said.

We ran from the study hall and down the second-floor corridor toward the auditorium, where we could look out the window in front. We almost ran into Miss McCallum, the math teacher.

"Just what do you boys think you're doing?" she said.

"We thought we saw something going on out front," I said. "We wanted to double-check."

"You can turn right around and go back to the classroom and finish your homework, or you'll be double-checking in the principal's office," Miss McCallum said.

Billy looked scared. I didn't think I should tell Old Lady McCallum anything. I wasn't sure why exactly, but I knew Miss Delaney wouldn't want me to.

"March," Miss McCallum said.

We went back to the classroom, and Old Lady McCallum sat at the front and watched us while Billy finished his math homework. I had to pretend I was doing my homework, or she'd have made me leave. And I didn't want to hang outside in the cold waiting for Billy. You weren't allowed to wait around inside the school without supervision. So I sat in the big silence and pretended to be calculating stuff while Billy struggled through the rest of his assignment.

"When you leave here," Miss McCallum said, "I want you to go straight down the stairs and out of the building. And no running in the corridors."

Billy said, "Yes, ma'am."

I nodded. We went out of the classroom and down the front stairs and out the front door. There was some wind. The flag was snapping on the flagpole in front of the school. On the other side of the wide front lawn, there was a robin's-egg blue Plymouth Coupe parked on the street. As we walked past it, Miss Delaney got out. She had on a plaid topcoat and a black beret.

"Bobby," she said to me, "could I talk to you and Billy for a moment?"

CHAPTER 4

"TELL me what you saw," Miss Delaney said.

"I didn't see nothing," Billy said.

"Bobby?" Miss Delaney said to me.

"You had an argument with a guy," I said.

"Was it you who yelled?"

"Yes."

"Thank you," Miss Delaney said.

I nodded.

"Did you tell anybody what you saw?" Miss Delaney said.

Billy shook his head.

"We won't tell nobody," Billy said.

"Bobby?" Miss Delaney said.

"Mum's the word," I said.

"Good. It's nothing, but it would be kind of embarrassing, I guess, if this got talked about."

I felt uneasy. It was very strange to talk this way with Miss Delaney.

"Do you need any help?" I said.

"No, Bobby. That's very sweet. But it's just someone I used to know and we had a little argument."

I didn't like it. I wanted to know more. But I didn't know how to ask.

"And you're gonna be okay?" I said.

"Yes. As long as we keep it a secret," Miss Delaney said, "I'll be fine."

We were all quiet for a moment, and then Miss Delaney leaned over and kissed Billy on the cheek and then me.

"Our secret," she said, and got in her car and drove away down Church Street.

"You smell her?" Billy said. "She was wearing some kind of perfume. You smell how she smelled?"

"She smelled good," I said.

"What'd she kiss us for?" Billy said

A gray Ford Tudor came around the corner from North Street and went down Church Street in the same direction as Miss Delaney. Billy and I watched it go until it was out of sight.

"You think that was him?" Billy said.

"I don't know," I said.

"You think she was telling us the truth?" Billy said.

"Not all of it," I said.

"Why do you think it's a secret?"

"I don't know."

"You think he was some kind of old boyfriend?" Billy said.

It was kind of exciting to think about Miss Delaney having a boyfriend. I didn't exactly like it. But I didn't not like it either.

"I don't know, Billy. I don't know who he was or what was going on except he grabbed her and she slapped him, and I yelled and she got away from him and came in the school."

"And he didn't follow her in?"

"No."

"Was Mr. Welch here?" Billy said.

"He usually is," I said.

Mr. Welch was the principal. The only man except the janitor in the school. He was a pretty big guy, and once when an older guy we were all scared of, Anthony Pimentel, had come in the school, Mr. Welch had taken him by the back of his collar, bum-rushed him down the stairs, and thrown him out the front door. None of us ever admitted it, but we were impressed as hell.

"You gonna tell anyone?" Billy said.

"We said we wouldn't."

"But maybe we should tell Mr. Welch," Billy said.

"We said we wouldn't."

Billy nodded.

"I don't want to get into trouble," Billy said.

"You keep your mouth shut," I said. "You almost never get into trouble."

"Yeah. Okay," Billy said. "Loose lips sink ships."

"I think we should keep an eye on her, though."

"An eye?" Billy said.

"Yeah, just stay ready, see what happens. Be alert, you know?"

"If we told the other guys, they could keep an eye on her too," Billy said.

"Not yet," I said. "We need help, we tell them. For now we just, like, stay alert."

"So what do you think's going on?" Billy said.

"I don't know yet," I said.

"Yet?"

I was quiet for a moment. Up behind us, the flag was still snapping in the breeze.

"I'll figure it out," I said.

I had a small brown GE radio in my bedroom and listened to it nearly every night. I listened to boxing from Madison Square Garden with Don Dunphy describing the fight. The ring announcer was Harry Ballough . . . The Fitch Band Wagon, with Dick Powell . . . "Don't dispair, use your head, save your hair, use Fitch Shampoo." . . . The Manhattan Merry Go Round, where I imagined myself actually going to the impossibly sophisticated clubs in Manhattan . . . Lux Radio Theater (Lux Presents Hollywood, with your host, Cecil B. DeMille) . . . And always the commercials: Get Wildwood Cream Oil, Charlie, start using it today . . . Ipana for the smile of beauty, Sal Hepatica for the smile of health . . . Serutan spelled backward in Nature's . . . more doctors smoke Camels than any other cigarette . . . On Boston radio there was a fifteen-minute show at noon that an announcer would introduce every day by saying, "Sit back, relax, and listen to Bing Sing." . . . like everybody else, I loved Bing Crosby . . . On network there was **The Jack Benny Program** with Mary Livingston, Phil Harris, Dennis Day, Rochester, and "yours truly, Don Wilson." It was originally sponsored by Jell-O (J-E-L-L-O), and later by Lucky Strikes (LS/MFT). Jack had a pet polar bear named Carmichael, who he kept in the cellar . . . For adventure the afternoon pro-

20

grams were good—Jack Armstrong, Don Winslow of the Navy, Hop Harrigan. . . . Afternoons I would listen to ball games, the Red Sox and the Braves . . . When a team was out of town there would be telegraph re-creations with Jim Britt or Tom Hussy reading the play-by-play off a telegraph setup and simulating a real play-by-play . . . For more grown-up listeners Big Town was good, Steve Wilson of the illustrated press and his girl-friend Lorelei Kilbourn: "Freedom of the press," Steve would say at the start of every program, "is a flaming sword, use it wisely, hold it high, guard it well." And "Mister District Attorney," "I Love a Mystery" Jack, Doc and Reggie always on some lost plateau somewhere.

CHAPTER 5

I had known Joanie Gibson all my life. We had met when we were three years old at somebody's birthday party. We had been all through school together, and even though she was a girl, we were friends.

Joanie was one of the first girls in class to get boobs. They weren't very big. But there they were. She had really nice eyes too. Very big eyes. Blue. The fact that she had boobs made her seem hot to us, but I also liked her. I wasn't exactly sure where *hot* ended and *like* began, and I didn't exactly know how to like a girl. On the other hand, I didn't exactly know how to deal with *hot* either . . . Besides, we were friends.

Nick used to meet her after school sometimes, and buy her a Coke at the Village Shop, and maybe walk her home. So we kind of thought of her as his girlfriend. But she was still my friend.

In bad weather, especially when it was raining and windy, I used to like to go down to the empty bandstand and sit in it alone, protected by the pointed roof, and look at the way the rain and the wind made the harbor look. I was doing it on the Saturday afternoon after I saw Miss Delaney and the guy. Usually the harbor was dotted with sails. But the weather was too lousy, and all the boats were bucking and tossing at their moorings. Close in, there were a lot of Herreshoff 12s, and Beetle Cats. The wind made the empty gray surface of the harbor ripple in an odd crisscross pattern, sort of like the surface of a wood file. Farther out were bigger boats, of which I knew very little.

A girl's voice said, "Are you thinking?"

I knew the voice.

"Sort of," I said.

"You sure do a lot of that, Bobby," Joanie Gibson said, and sat down beside me facing the water.

She had on saddle shoes and thick white socks and a camel's hair coat.

"There's a lot to think about," I said.

"What are you thinking about now?" Joanie said.

"I don't know."

23

"I get like that sometimes," Joanie said. "I mean, my mind is sort of out there moving around, but I don't quite know what it's doing."

That was right. That was exactly how it was. Her too. I didn't know what to say.

"It's nice here," she said. "Under the roof, out of the bad weather, warm coat. And out on the water it's kind of rough and mean and cold, and we're not on it."

"I could be on it," I said. "Sheet in one hand, tiller in the other, running before the wind. My hair blowing back like in the movies."

"You have a crew cut."

"So I'll let it grow and then I'll go out in a storm."

"You're embarrassed," Joanie said. "Aren't you?

"Huh?"

"You always try to be funny when you're embarrassed."

"What am I embarrassed about?" I said.

"Maybe embarrassed isn't the right word," Joanie said. "It's more like you're much smarter than anybody else, and you don't want people to know it. So you always joke around."

"So what am I supposed to do," I said, "walk around, *I'm smart, I'm smart* all the time?"

"No, just don't pretend you're not."

"It's not good to be too smart," I said.

"It's not good to be too stupid either," Joanie said.

I didn't know what to say. I didn't like that. I always knew what to say. Way out past the harbor mouth I could see a big schooner tacking back and forth across the wind, beating its way back into the harbor.

"I'm smart too," Joanie said. "And I've known you all my life. I thought maybe we could talk."

"About what?" I said.

"About why you like to sit in the rain and look at the water," Joanie said.

I nodded.

"We could talk about that," I said.

Joanie smiled at me.

"Good," she said.

CHAPTER 6

THERE was a balcony above the Eastfield High School gym and I was sitting in it watching the high school varsity practice.

Coach threw the ball to one of the guards.

"Weave," he said.

The five began to move. The man with the ball dribbled in one direction, a man without the ball came toward him. The dribbler went inside the other guy and left the ball for him and continued into the corner. The new dribbler went inside the next guy and left the ball for him and continued to the corner. They did this for a long time. Weaving past each other, and handing off so that the ball was always in the middle of the court and always in motion.

Then Coach said, "Sherm, take it to the hoop."

Sherm was a blocky, muscular little guard. He came

out of the corner, in the weave, and when he reached mid-court, he took the handoff and broke sharply for the basket right off the backside of the guy that just handed him the ball and went in and laid the ball up.

"Good," Coach said. "Weave again."

And they went back to it. Each guy took his turn driving for a layup off the weave.

After a time Coach said, "Okay Bart, start a roll."

This time when Sherm came around and got the ball, Bart, the biggest guy on the team, turned and headed for the basket. Sherm passed it to him. And Bart took a layup.

"Lou," Coach said.

And they ran that play over and over with different men taking the layup. I had a notebook and some pencils. But I didn't use them. I just watched. Taking notes always kept me from learning stuff. I could write down things later if I had to.

"Okay," Coach said. "Give and go. Out of the weave. Sherm, start it."

So they went back to the weave, only this time as Sherm dribbled the ball toward midcourt and Bart approached him, Sherm stopped and passed the ball to Bart. Bart passed it right back to him and broke for the basket. They did this forever and when they finally stopped, all of them were puffing hard and shining with sweat.

"Okay, first unit," Coach said. "Foul shots. Other end. Twenty each and I'll be keeping an eye on you. Second unit come on in here and give me a weave."

The starters went up the other end and began to shoot free throws. One guy shot. One guy retrieved, the other guys shot around. All of the guys but Sherm shot overhand. Sherm did the underhand free throw. And he was pretty good at it. I wasn't much of a foul-shooter. But I'd rather miss than shoot underhand.

CHAPTER 7

WE were in the school yard and I was showing the Owls what I'd learned.

"You always go inside the guy you're handing off to," I said. "That's what Coach says. Always inside."

"Away from the defender," Nick said.

"It work against a zone?" Russell asked.

"Don't know. They haven't run plays for a zone yet," I said.

"You going back to watch more practice?" Manny said.

"Yeah."

"Maybe they'll say something about a zone," Nick said.

Russell was holding the basketball.

"They'll say throw it in to me," he said. "For the pivot shot."

He demonstrated the pivot shot.

"Kurland turns," he announced, "shoots, scores."

The ball clanked off the rim.

"But Russell doesn't," Nick said.

On North Street, across from the side of the school where we were practicing, a gray Ford Tudor was parked. It had a red stripe along the side of it. Billy saw me looking and looked too.

"That the one?" Billy said.

I shook my head at him, *Don't talk about it.*

"The other one had a red stripe. I remember seeing it."

"They probably all have a red stripe," I said.

"What are you guys talking about?" Nick said.

"New Ford over there. You like it?"

"Sure," Nick said. "After five years looking at the '41s."

"I'm gonna take a closer look," I said.

"Hell," Nick said. "Is it the first one you've seen?"

"I seen some go by," I said, "but this is the first one I could look close at."

I walked toward the car. There was someone in it. My stomach was scared. As I got closer, I looked at the license plate and repeated the number to myself, trying to remember it. A man got out of the car. It was him. He was wearing a trench coat today, and a tweed cap like long-shoremen wear. But it was him.

He said, "What can I do for you, young man?"

"I was just looking at your car," I said. "It's nice."

"Thanks. Anything else?"

I kept looking at him, trying to figure him out.

"It's a '46," I said, "right?"

"It is."

"They make a coupe?" I asked. "Or a convertible?"

"I am not a car salesman," the man said.

"I was just asking," I said.

"Fine," he said. "Now you've seen it, run along."

The other Owls had stopped practice and were watching us.

"I'm not doing anything," I said.

"If you don't run along," the man said, "I'll give you reason to."

There was something in his voice, like a piece of broken glass. I nodded and turned, and walked back to the other guys.

CHAPTER 8

WHEN the bell rang, Miss Delaney said, "Bobby Murphy, could you stay a moment after class, please?"

"I think she's hot for you," Russell murmured as he stood up.

"Like hell," Nick said. "It's me she wants."

When the classroom emptied, Miss Delaney came and sat down on the edge of my desk.

"I saw you yesterday," she said. "Talking to the man in the gray Ford."

I nodded. The way she was sitting pulled her dress tight over her thighs. I tried not to look. I imagined what she might look like with her clothes off. Then I felt sort of like I was bad to think about that.

"What did you say?"

"I said I liked his new car, wanted to get a closer look at it."

"Why did you go talk to him?"

"He's the guy you had an argument with," I said.

"So?"

"So I wanted a better look at him," I said.

"Because?"

"Because if you're in trouble, I want to be able to help."

Miss Delaney looked at me without speaking for a moment. I thought about her thighs. I wondered if it was a sin to think about her with her clothes off. I hoped it was only a venial sin. I mean, guys thought about stuff like that.

"You will get me in trouble ," Miss Delaney said, "unless you simply forget anything you may have seen."

"He seems kind of scary to me," I said. "I'm just trying to figure him out."

Miss Delaney smiled. It didn't seem like a happy smile to me.

"You think you can figure anything out," she said, "don't you?"

"Sooner or later," I said.

"That's because you're fourteen," Miss Delaney said.

"No it's not," I said. "It's because I'm smart."

She smiled again, the same smile with no happiness in it.

"You're both," she said. "But please, as a favor to me, please stay out of this. You can't help. I doubt that you could even understand it. All you can do is cause trouble for me."

"I don't want to cause you any trouble," I said.

"Then promise me," she said. "To tell no one about any of this, and to leave me and that man alone."

"Maybe you should tell Mr. Welch about it," I suggested.

He had, after all, given the bum's rush to Anthony Pimentel.

"Oh my God, no," Miss Delaney said.

"He threw Anthony Pimentel out of the school once," I said.

"Promise me," she said, "that you'll stay out of this."

I nodded.

"And that you won't tell anyone," she said, "including Mr. Welch."

I nodded.

"I have your word?"

I nodded.

"Okay," she said. "I trust you to keep your word."

I nodded again. Nodding didn't count. If you didn't actually *say* the promise, I always figured you didn't have to keep it. Miss Delaney put her hand on my shoulder for a moment as she looked at me. Then she stood and smoothed her skirt, and walked back toward her desk.

"That's all, Bobby," she said. "Thank you."

I stood and walked out of the classroom. I felt a little funny, like my head was disconnected. The corridor was empty. At the end of the school day people didn't hang around. It was worse than she said. I could still hear the sound of broken glass in that man's voice. There was something going on here that I didn't get. But I would. I was smart.

I could too figure it out.

CHAPTER 9

"**I** thought you'd be here," Joanie said.

"What made you think so?" I asked.

Joanie stepped up onto the bandstand and sat on the bench beside me.

"Because the weather is terrible and everybody else is inside," she said.

"I like bad weather," I said.

"Why?"

"I don't know," I said. "It's kind of exciting, I guess."

"Do you come here to think?" Joanie said.

"Sometimes."

"What are you thinking about now?" she asked.

"You," I said.

"I mean before I came," Joanie said. "Were you thinking about a problem?"

"Yeah."

"What?"

"Can't tell you now," I said.

"Oh."

We were quiet.

"It's not you," I said to Joanie. "I gave my word I wouldn't tell."

"You're making me die to know what it is," she said.

"I can't," I said. "I gave my word."

She nodded.

"Stuff like that matters to you," she said. "Keeping your word and stuff."

"Yes."

There was no wind this time. Just a hard rain coming straight down on the calm water of the harbor.

"It's hard being a kid," Joanie said. "Grown-ups tell you how easy it is. But it's not."

"Kids problems don't seem serious to grown-ups," I said.

"But they are serious to kids," Joanie said. "Getting grades. Being popular. Having friends."

"Making a team," I said. "Being brave."

"Being brave?" Joanie asked.

"Yeah. Boys are supposed to be brave."

"You think about that?"

"Sure," I said. "I want to be brave and, uh, you

know . . ." I rolled my hands, trying to find the right word. "Like a knight . . . honorable."

"Honorable?" Joanie said.

I nodded. The rain sound was steady on the roof of the bandstand. It made a sort of hushed sound around us as it fell. And the wet smell mixed with the salt smell and everything seemed very exciting.

"You know," I said, "like Philip Marlowe."

"Who?"

"Guy in a book," I said.

Joanie nodded.

"You read a lot of books, Bobby."

"I like to read," I said.

"What about your problem that you promised not to tell?"

"I promised not to," I said.

"Is one of your friends mad at you?"

"No."

"I hate when one of my friends gets mad at me," Joanie said.

"I know," I said. "I always say it doesn't matter. But it does."

"It makes me feel scared," Joanie said.

I nodded.

"Are you ever scared, Bobby?" she said.

I wanted to say no in the worst way, but I opened my mouth and heard myself say, "Yes."

"What of?"

"People being mad at me, I guess. Not being, you know, nobody liking me."

I couldn't believe it. I never even talked to *myself* about stuff like this.

"Let's make a promise," Joanie said.

"What?"

"Let's promise we'll never be mad at each other."

"No matter what?" I said.

"No matter what," Joanie said. "We will always be each other's friend."

"I never had a friend, except you, who was a girl," I said.

"And I never had a friend, except you, who was a boy," Joanie said. "Promise?"

Sitting in the bandstand with the weather all around us, I looked at her for a long time.

Then I said, "Promise."

CHAPTER 10

BILLY sat beside me in the back row in homeroom.

"Was it him?" Billy whispered to me.

"Yeah."

"He recognize you?"

"I don't think so."

"What'd you tell him?"

"I said I liked his car."

"What are you going to do now?" Billy whispered.

"Billy," Miss Delaney said. "Will you swap seats with Manny, please, for the rest of class?"

Miss Delaney knew that Manny rarely said anything, and putting him between me and Billy would quiet us all down. But she didn't break the Owls up, just shuffled us around a little.

"Thank you," Miss Delaney said when the swap was completed.

When school was out, we went to the basketball court in the yard.

"Okay," I said. "Let's do that weave again to warm up."

"Okay, Coach," Russell said.

"You been over to the high school again this week?" Nick asked.

"I got some new stuff," I said. "After we warm up."

"They warm up at the high school?" Manny said.

I was always a little startled when he spoke, he was so silent so much of the time.

"Course," I said.

Manny smiled and loped into the corner with the basketball and started the weave.

"Inside," I said to Russell. "Inside the guy you're handing off to."

"Screw you," Russell said. "I started this team. I'll go where I want."

"You want to go to the tourney or not?" I said.

"We got to get better, Russell," Nick said. "We stunk up the gym when we played the JVs that time."

"Yeah, yeah," Russell said.

And the weave continued.

"Now," I said when we were done weaving, "we're going to work on screens."

"We don't need screens," Russell said. "Until spring."

"Very funny," I said. "Manny, say you got the ball over there. Now you pass it to me and run over here and stop. You got to be set to screen for me. A moving screen is a foul. Okay, come on . . . pass me the ball . . . and run over . . . stop. . . . Now I got the ball, I can either dribble past the screen and lose the guy guarding me . . . or if I can't lose him, or they switch, I can pull up behind Manny and hit the set shot."

I put up a one-hand shot, which hit the front of the rim and bounced away.

"Work even better," Russell said, "if you hit the shot."

"You'll get your chance," I told him.

We practiced screens for the rest of the afternoon. I noticed that a lot of the plays the JVs ran had people moving without the ball and getting the ball passed to them when they were behind the screen. And I'd heard Coach talk about a double screen, but I didn't quite see what that was. Today we'd just keep it simple. Pass the ball and set the screen.

After practice when I was walking home with Manny, I saw the car again, parked on Church Street this time, in front of the school. I kept my head down and didn't look at it as we went by.

CHAPTER 11

JOANIE invited Nick to go to a party with her at the Boat Club. I was glad I didn't have to go. I couldn't dance. We'd all gone to dancing class except Manny, and we all liked pressing against the girls. What we weren't interested in was all the crap about who led who, and how you asked a young lady to dance and *la di da.* But if Joanie had asked me to the party and I'd had to dance, I would have been embarrassed.

Joanie had asked me what I thought about her inviting Nick. I had said he was a good guy. She said she thought he was really cute. I kind of didn't like that. But she wasn't my girlfriend. We were pals.

"You think he'll go?" Joanie had asked me.

"Sure," I said.

Nick was the first one of us to have a regular date, and the first one of us to ever be invited to the Boat Club.

The rest of us sort of followed Nick and Joanie at a distance, and hung around outside. I don't know quite why. Wanted to see what was up, I guess.

The thing was, I felt funny about it. I felt funny about her asking Nick and funny about feeling funny about it. I didn't exactly wish she hadn't asked him. And I didn't exactly wish she had asked me. I guess I wished she hadn't asked anyone and had, instead, come down and sat on the deserted bandstand with me.

"You think they might do something?" Russell said to the group of us.

"Joanie and Nick?" Billy said.

"Yeah. You think he might get a good-night kiss?"

"She seems pretty hot," Billy said.

"Maybe more than a good-night kiss," Russell said.

I didn't like the conversation. But I couldn't think of any way to complain about it. We talked all the time about what you could get a girl to do. As far as I knew, none of us had actually gotten a girl to do much of anything. But it didn't slow the conversation any. If we couldn't speak of what we had done, we could talk a lot about what we would do. Or would like to do.

That's all Russell and Billy were doing. So why did it bother me? We hung around across the street from the Boat Club. We could hear music and see lights. But we couldn't really keep track of what was going on. Beyond the Boat Club was a private beach where the waves washed softly up.

There was a roadhouse up on Route 6 where things we couldn't imagine were supposed to go on, and now and then we would sneak up there and try to peek in the windows. But the windows were all tightly covered and we could never see anything. And we were always almost breathless with what we imagined could be going on beyond our ability to see.

I felt sort of like that now. And the more I couldn't see, the more my stomach tightened up, and the more I felt feverish, and the harder it was to swallow.

"You're the brains," Russell said to me. "You think she's hot?"

"Not for me," I said.

"Who is?" Billy said. "Except maybe Miss Delaney."

I walked away toward the beach.

"Miss Delaney's hot for us all," Russell said.

I kept walking.

"Hey," Russell called. "Where you going?"

I didn't answer.

"Hey, what's the matter with you?" Russell said.

"Let him be," Manny said. "He wants to look at the water, let him look at the water."

"Don't you wanna see what's going to happen?" Russell said.

"Maybe he'll kiss her good night," Billy said. "You don't want to see that?"

I kept walking.

Behind me I heard Billy say, "What the hell's wrong with him?"

"He's pretty weird sometimes," Russell said.

There was enough moon, so I could see okay. At the edge of the sand where the waves broke, there was a little white foam drifting. I watched it as it slid back out with the receding wave, and re-formed when the wave came gently up the sand again.

CHAPTER 12

WE had our first game against a JV team from Hartfield in the gym at Hartfield High School. There weren't many people watching. But it was a real game, with a referee. There was no one on their team as tall as Russell. He got the tip. We went right away into our weave and the Hartfield guys looked a little confused. We kept at it until Russell's man began to anticipate the weave and then Russell faked coming toward the man with the ball (who was me), and broke suddenly behind his man toward the basket. I got him the ball and Russell hit the layup. It was pretty clear that if we could get Russell the ball near the basket, he could shoot a layup over anyone that they had guarding him.

In the second half we had a big lead and we started

experimenting with Nick driving for the basket off the weave, and Billy shooting set shots behind a screen. Manny wasn't as tall as Russell, but he worked harder and got a lot of rebounds. He always looked to pass out, but at halftime I had told him to start putting some of them up. And in the second half he did.

We won by a lot, and hitchhiking home afterward, we were really up, throwing the ball around, telling each other how good we were.

"What kind of trophy they give when you win the tourney?" Russell said.

"They're going to give you the ball hog trophy," Nick said."You shoot every time you get the ball."

"You mean I score every time," Russell said.

"I didn't see the ball so long," Billy said,"I almost forgot how to play."

"I could see that," Manny said.

"Hey," Billy said."How many points you get?"

A pickup truck stopped and the driver said we could ride in the back if we wanted. We jumped in.

As we rattled around in the back of the truck, I said,"You know why we won?"

"Because we're the class of the freakin' league," Russell said.

"Because they didn't play any defense at all," I said."They didn't know how to defend the weave. So they just gave up on it. They didn't fight for rebounds. They didn't have anybody to guard Russell. And all any of them wanted to do was heave the ball at the basket."

"So you're saying we won because they were crappy," Nick said.

"I'm saying that we won because we were better than they were," I said. "But it doesn't mean we're good yet."

"We could use a couple more guys," Manny said. "I was sucking air by the end."

"Not me," Russell said.

"That's because all you did was shoot layups," Billy told him. "Manny was working his ass off getting rebounds."

"Don't want to tire out your big scorer," Russell said.

The truck let us off on Route 6 at the corner of Main Street.

"You know anybody else who can play?" I asked. "That we can stand to play with?"

"Some of the older guys can play," Billy said.

"They don't want to play with us," I said.

"And anybody else," Nick said, "we can't stand."

"So it's just us, I guess. We gotta be sure and get in good condition."

"Hell, we practice every day," Russell said.

"Maybe we'll need to do some sprints too," I said. "You know, up and down the court?"

"Sprints?" Russell asked.

"Need to be strong at the end of the game," I said.

"What if somebody gets hurt?" Billy said. "And we don't have any other guys?"

"We're screwed," I said.

I read the newspaper every day. I didn't pay too much attention to the news. In the summer I went straight to the sports page and read the box scores. . . . Tommy Holmes had a great year for the Braves in 1945. Hit .352 and led the league in home runs with twenty-eight. The Braves finished in fourth place that year. The Red Sox with everyone still in the service finished seventh in the American League and an outfielder named Johnny Lazor was their leading hitter at .310. But the next year, with Williams and the others back, they won the pennant and Ted hit .342 . . . We had a pro football team those years. The Boston Yanks had Boley Dancewicz and Paul Governelli at quarterback. Babe Dimancheff was the main runner. Rocco Canale played guard and there was a kick returner named Sonny Karnofsky. The team was owned by Ted Collins, who everybody knew was Kate Smith's manager. The Boston Yanks played in Fenway Park sometimes, and were never very good . . . I felt that studying the sports page was more or less a responsibility; the funnies were pure entertainment. There was Alley Oop and his girlfriend Oola, with their pet dinosaur Dinny . . . There was L'il Abner, and Blondie, and Ella Cinders and Terry & The Pirates, and Red Ryder . . . Comic books were a longer form, more complex. I especially liked Batman and Robin, and Captain America and Bucky, and of course the print ads for Chesterfield cigarettes and Seagram's whiskey and the delicious meals you could make with canned ham and peaches . . . Another step up the intellectual ladder was LIFE Magazine, which came out once a week. It had wonderful pictures of everything that Americans cared about, and some great text and photo features on things like "Married Vets Return to College," and "LIFE Goes to a Sorority Party." There were always a few pictures of nice-looking girls changing clothes . . . There were whole series of writing and pictures on things like the renaissance . . . And "Life Goes to the Movies," which was a sort of capsule presentation of current movies with still photos from the movies, a magazine version of the Lux Hollywood Theater. LIFE always made me proud to be American.

CHAPTER 13

IT was a bright Saturday afternoon and no one was around. I walked down to the harbor and looked at the bandstand. It was empty. I went on down the hill past it and out to the end of the longest wharf, and sat on the stone surface and looked at the water.

Nick and I were a little ill at ease these days. Neither one of us said anything, but I figured it must have something to do with Joanie. I know it did for me. And I knew Russell was kind of PO'd because he thought the Owls were his team, and he didn't like me doing all the coaching. I didn't like it either, but there wasn't anyone else to do it, and we had to do something if we were going to get anywhere in the state tournament. Part of me doubted that we would. It was the part that was sort of separate from the rest of me, that knew the stuff that I didn't want to know.

That part knew why I had come down here past the bandstand.

Looking straight down into the greenish water, I could see small fish moving about the base of the dock. Much too small to catch. It was too late in the year to fish, anyway. I wondered if people didn't fish after Labor Day because the fish went somewhere, or if it was just because people thought it was too cold to sit out there with a line. Or maybe that was just the way it was done. The grown-up world was filled with stuff that you did because that's the way it was done.

The sun was behind me and to my right as I sat looking at the water. I saw her shadow before I saw her.

"Can I sit and stare at the water too?" Joanie said.

"It's not my water," I said.

She sat beside me. Her hair was shiny and smelled nice, like she'd just washed it.

"Nick says he thinks you're mad about him going to the Boat Club party with me."

"I'm not mad," I said. "He's your boyfriend."

"No," Joanie said. "He's not."

Something jumped inside me.

"He says he is."

"I can't help that," Joanie said. "But I am not his girl-friend."

"So why did you invite him to the party?"

"He's cute, and he's kind of nice," she answered. "He isn't grabby or anything."

I nodded. Two gulls landed near us and looked at us. In the summer, when we fished, we'd throw them a piece of bait, or maybe a small fish.

"But I'm not his girlfriend," Joanie said.

I nodded again.

"So why are you mad?"

"I told you," I said, "I'm not mad."

"We promised never to be mad at each other," Joanie said.

I nodded.

"And we promised always to be each other's friend," she said.

I nodded again. Our feet dangled over the edge of the dock, side by side. Hers were crossed at the ankles. She had on her saddle shoes again. I was wearing the thick-soled oxblood-colored shoes with two eyelets that I liked.

"Did we promise not to lie to each other?"

"I don't think so."

"I think we should," Joanie said. "I mean, how are we going to be each other's friend always, if we lie?"

"You think I'm lying?" I said.

Joanie nodded her head slowly. I smiled at her.

"Damn," I said.

She cocked her head a little and widened her eyes and shrugged.

"Promise?" she said.

"Promise," I said.

The two gulls got tired of waiting, and gave up and flew off.

"So," Joanie said. "Are you mad at me?"

"No."

"Nick?"

"No."

"But you're mad about something."

"I'm jealous," I said.

It came out before I knew it was going to, and now that it was out, there was no way to put it back.

"Did you wish I'd asked you?" Joanie said.

"I don't know. I know I didn't like it. I know I kept thinking about you in there. I thought, What if they are doing stuff?"

"You mean like kissing?" Joanie asked. "Making out?"

"Yes."

My voice sounded hoarse to me. The sky seemed much higher than it had and the harbor seemed bigger. Across the harbor the neck seemed really far.

"I asked Nick because he's very nice," Joanie said. "He doesn't even joke around or talk dirty the way Russell does. He's very polite."

I nodded.

"I've never made out with anybody," Joanie said.

I took a big breath. The ocean air was clean and bright. The neck didn't seem so far away.

"Me either," I said.

CHAPTER 14

THERE was a substitute teacher for Miss Delaney on Monday and Tuesday. We tortured her until Miss Delaney came back on Wednesday. There were some bruises showing on her face.

"I fell down the stairs," she told us. "I just tripped and fell."

"You drunk, Miss Delaney?" Russell said.

Everyone laughed, including Miss Delaney. It looked to me like when she laughed, it was uncomfortable.

"Sadly," she said with a smile, "I was not."

After class I hung back, and when no one else was in the room I went to the desk where Miss Delaney was sitting marking something in her rank book.

She didn't look up.

"Did he do something?" I asked.

"Who?" she said.

"That guy," I said. "The one I saw you with."

She looked up at me.

"Bobby," she said slowly, "it is none of your business."

"I just want to help," I said.

"You can help by saying nothing more about it, to me, or to anyone else," Miss Delaney said, "as you promised."

"I'll bet it was him," I said.

"No," Miss Delaney said. "It was not."

She looked straight at me. Neither of us said anything else. I didn't know what to do. Finally, I turned and walked out of the room.

Outside in the school yard the Owls were already practicing. They were running up and down the court passing the ball back and forth, not dribbling at all. It was Russell's idea. We got to work on our wind and our passing at the same time. The object was not to take more than two and a half steps with the ball. It was pretty cold, and it was getting dark earlier and earlier. But as long as it didn't snow, we were all right, even if we had to play with too many clothes on.

Billy dropped out of the running and came over to me.

"You talk to her?" he asked me.

"Yeah."

"Did he do it?" Billy said. "That guy?"

"She said no."

"What'd you say?"

"I said I thought he did."

"She get mad?"

"Kind of," I said. "I told her we just wanted to help."

"What'd she say about that?"

"She said it wasn't him and she kind of gave me the evil eye, you know?"

"Oh yeah," Billy said. "The mean look. She's usually so nice, you can't friggin' believe it when she gives you that mean look. So what are you gonna do?"

"I don't know," I said.

"You guys gonna practice?" Russell said. "Or you just gonna chew the fat all the rest of the day?"

"Maybe we should tell somebody," Billy said.

"We promised not to," I said.

Billy shrugged.

"Hey," Russell yelled. "You too good to practice?"

Russell liked being in charge. He fired the ball at us and it bounced off the school wall and rolled away. I went after it, and got it and dribbled it back toward the practice area.

"Okay," I said. "Watch yourself. Murphy's on the move."

CHAPTER 15

THANK God it was raining hard after school the next day, so I didn't have to practice. Instead, I waited in the stairwell until Joanie came down the stairs with her girlfriends. We looked at each other.

As she passed she said, "Bandstand?"

I nodded. She went on with her girlfriends and I walked down to the bandstand with my Owls jacket buttoned up, and the rain falling hard on my bare head. I was in the bandstand for maybe ten minutes when Joanie arrived in a raincoat with a big green scarf over her hair. It was dark. The rain clouds seemed only a few feet above the bandstand. The harbor water was almost black. There was no one else in sight.

"Our kind of day," Joanie said when she sat down.

" 'Stormy Weather,' " I said.

She smiled.

"What's wrong?" Joanie said.

I got up and walked to the railing and looked down at the empty harbor.

"I don't know who else to talk to," I said.

"I'm glad it's me," Joanie said.

The weather was so thick, I couldn't see across the harbor. The neck was invisible.

"I promised I wouldn't tell anybody," I said.

Joanie didn't say anything. She sat with her knees together and her hands in her lap. She was wearing white rubber rain boots.

"I gotta tell somebody about it," I said. "I gotta figure out what to do."

"I'll help," Joanie said.

I turned back toward Joanie. I was so close to the edge of the bandstand that I could feel the rain on the back of my jacket.

"But a man's supposed to keep his word," I said. "You're supposed to do what you said you'd do."

Joanie looked at me for a long time without saying anything.

"I think," she said finally, "that a man does what he thinks is the right thing to do, even if it means breaking his word."

We looked at each other without speaking for a while. Then I said, "Somebody's trying to hurt Miss Delaney."

"What do you mean?" Joanie said. "Who?"

"There's a guy," I said. "I've seen him . . ." And I told her what I had seen, and what Miss Delaney had said.

"Is it some sort of love thing?" Joanie asked.

"Miss Delaney?"

"Sure. Teachers have boyfriends and stuff, don't they?"

"But if he loves her, why is he mean to her?" I said.

"It happens a lot," she said. "Remember that movie with Bette Davis?"

"No."

"You know, when George Brent was the husband?"

"I didn't see it," I said.

"Anyway, I'll bet it's some kind of love business," Joanie said. "Maybe we should tell Mr. Welch."

"Miss Delaney says it will get her in trouble."

"Mr. Welch isn't so bad," Joanie said.

"No," I said. "But doesn't he have to do what the town tells him to do?"

"I guess."

"You know what they're like," I said.

"Yes."

"So we'll have to figure out how to help her ourselves."

"Are the other Owls in on this?" Joanie said.

"Just Billy," I said. "But they'll help us if I tell them."

"So what are we going to do?" she said.

"We probably gotta start by finding out who this guy is," I said.

"How?"

"I got his license plate number," I said.

"And how do you find out whose it is?" Joanie asked. "We're kids. We can't just call up and ask whose plate is this."

"I know," I said. "They won't tell us. You know any grown-ups we could trust?"

"No," Joanie said. "And if I did, I think they won't tell you even if you're a grown-up. Unless you're a cop or something."

"We'll have to follow him," I said.

"How will you even find him to follow?"

"We'll have to follow Miss Delaney," I said. "And if he comes to see her again, we'll follow him."

"How will you follow him if he's in his car?" Joanie said.

"I don't know," I said. "We'll just have to do the best we can."

"And then what?" Joanie said.

I felt good. We had a plan. Joanie was going to help.

"Then we'll figure out the next step," I said.

CHAPTER 16

"**WHAT** about basketball?" Russell said.

All five of us were squeezed into a booth at the Village Shop, drinking Orange Crush.

"The weather's so crappy," I said, "we won't be able to practice much anyway. We know our plays. We can do our wind sprints on our own. And we can play the games on Saturday morning."

"What about Miss Delaney telling us not to get involved?" Billy said.

"We gotta," I said. "She's in trouble and she's got nobody to help her."

"Geez," Nick said. "You sound like Boston Blackie."

"The other day in class," I said. "You saw how she was all beat up."

"Maybe she really did fall down the stairs," Manny said.

I shook my head. "No," I said. "She needs help. You guys can help or not. But I'm going to do something."

"Anybody else know about this?" Russell asked.

"Joanie," I said.

"Joanie Gibson?" Nick said.

"Yeah."

"That means Nick is ready to go," Russell said.

Billy and Manny laughed. Nick didn't say anything. Neither did I.

"So, who's in?" Russell said.

"Me," Manny answered.

Billy nodded.

"I'm in," he said.

"You in, Nick?" Russell said.

"Sure," Nick said.

"Hell," Russell said. "It's unanimous. Owls Detective Agency on the job . . . We'll win the tourney *and* save Miss Delaney."

We spent most of the rest of the afternoon planning our strategy. It was fun. Like war games when we were little kids. Or cops and robbers. And the fact that it was real and not a game made it more fun. When we got through and left the Village Shop, Nick and I dropped back from the other three.

"You trying to cut me out with Joanie?" Nick said.

"She says she's not your girlfriend," I said.

"I say she is," Nick said.

"Well," I said, "she's not my girlfriend."

"So what is she?"

"My friend," I answered.

"She's a girl," Nick said.

"I like her," I said. "She's smart and she's funny and she's nice."

"Yeah, and she's my girl," Nick said. "I want you to stay away from her."

"I don't want to be her boyfriend," I told him.

I wasn't so sure of that, in fact. I'd never been anyone's boyfriend, and I wasn't sure what it would mean to be one.

"Well, just keep it that way," Nick said.

"But I'll still be her friend," I said.

Nick nodded.

"Like I said," he answered.

CHAPTER 17

WE knew Miss Delaney lived on the second floor of a two-family on Water Street. The plan was to hang out near her house and watch and see what we could see. The man showed up there after a few nights, but he went straight in her door and we had no way to know what was going on. When he left, he got right in his car and drove away. We had no way to follow him.

"This is no good," Nick said the next night. "We're not doing Miss Delaney any good standing out here. We can't see or hear anything. And if the guy shows up, he drives off when he's through and we can't follow him."

"Maybe she screams," Russell said, "and we hear her, we can all run in."

"And what," Billy said, "fight the guy? He's a man, for cripe's sake."

"There's five of us," I said.

"And what?" Nick said. "You think you're Robin the Boy Wonder? You've seen the guy. You think we can fight him?"

I shrugged. It was cold. We stood around in the dark on Water Street until we had to go home. Nobody showed up.

Nobody showed up the next night, or the next, and each night was cold.

On the fifth night when nothing happened Manny said, "This is a waste of time."

Manny said so little that when he did say something, it always sounded kind of important.

"We're not helping anybody," Manny said.

"And we got a game tomorrow," Russell pointed out. "We should be getting to bed early instead of standing around in the dark, like a bunch of dorks."

"The Edenville Dorks," Russell said.

Everybody laughed.

"The hell with this," Nick said. "I'm going home."

"Me too," Billy said.

They began to drift away.

"You coming, Bobby?" Russell asked me.

"Nope."

Russell stood still for a minute and then shook his head.

"See you tomorrow," he said, and went after the other guys.

Standing alone in the dark on the empty street, I felt like a fool. My eyes teared a little. What a jerk, I thought. You thought it would be like the movies. Stake out the house and in two minutes the bad guys show up and the action starts. The movies didn't show you the hero standing around in the cold hour after hour, needing to take a leak, wishing he had something to eat. Getting nowhere. Seeing nothing. Doing no good. And what about friendship? All those war movies where guys were heroically dying for each other. A little boredom. A little cold weather and the Owls flew away in the night. The hell with them. But I couldn't say the hell with them. We had a game tomorrow. I looked at the blank ungrateful front of the two-family house where Miss Delaney lived. There were things you can't do anything about. The thought scared me. It made me feel kind of helpless. But there it was. I turned and headed home.

CHAPTER 18

ON Saturday morning, at the high school, we played a team from Alton. The Alton team was a lot better than the guys we played before. They had a coach, and they knew how to play. But except for number 22, they couldn't throw the ball in the ocean.

Russell was, as usual, taller than the other center, and we were able to get him the ball close to the basket. Billy was hitting his outside set shot from behind the screens we set up for him. And Manny was getting his share of the rebounds.

But number 22 was keeping them in the game. He was one of those kids who probably shaved in the seventh grade. He had muscles. He was fast. Sometimes he would shoot a layup with his left hand. He was deadly from the outside. But if you played up on him to stop the outside shot, he would drive past you and go in for the layup.

We tried double-teaming him. But they would spread the floor and he would pass the ball to the open man the minute he was double-teamed. Then we would run back to guard that guy and they'd pass back to number 22, and he was one on one again before we could get back to him.

In the middle of the second half he had eighteen points, and Alton was beating us by four, when we called a timeout.

We were all breathing hard. We had no subs. We played the full game every time. But we weren't breathing as hard as we used to.

"We gotta do something about twenty-two," I said.

"Double-teaming him doesn't work," Russell said.

"We gotta put someone on him that has no other assignment. Whoever guards twenty-two doesn't have to score or rebound or help bring the ball up. He just stays with twenty-two."

"Worth a try," Manny said.

"Who?" Billy said.

"Nick's the best athlete on the team," I said.

Everybody nodded. All of us, including Nick, knew that was true.

"I'll take him," Nick said.

"Okay," I said. "We'll basically forget about you on offense. If you can score too, fine. But your job is to stay right in twenty-two's face the rest of the way."

"Gonna ruin your scoring average," Russell said.

"Then it'll be down with yours," Nick said.

"Don't get caught fouling him," I told him. "We got nobody else, remember. You foul out and we're screwed."

Nick nodded.

"And if he wants to pass, let him," I said. "What we want is the ball out of his hands."

"I'm on him," Nick said. "He's a dead man."

We brought the ball in at midcourt. I got it to Manny in the corner, who passed into Russell, who shot over his man with a little turn around. We were within two.

Number 22 normally brought the ball up, and when Alton passed in to him under their own basket, Nick was right up on him, in a crouch, arms extended, eyes focused on the middle of 22's stomach. It's nearly impossible to fake with your stomach. It has to go where you go. Number 22 tried to go around him, and Nick kept his feet moving and stayed in front of him. He tried the other way, dribbling with his left hand. Nick stayed with him. Number 22 got frustrated and ran straight into Nick, and the referee called him for charging and we got the ball.

I brought it up, and when we got to the top of the key, we went into a four-man weave without Nick. Nick was staying next to 22. Which meant that 22 had to guard him, so the rest of us were four on four. Billy put up another set shot. It rimmed out, and Manny got the rebound and put it back up, and we were tied.

And that's how it stayed. Back and forth so that with two minutes left we were still tied. Number 22 had not scored in more than five minutes, and he was clearly tired. During breaks in the game he would stand bent over with his hands on his knees. Nick bothered him so much that Alton had someone else bring the ball up. Nick stayed up on 22. Once 22 tried to cut to the basket without the ball and Nick blocked his way. Then 22 shoved him. Nick stepped away smiling.

"Now, now," he said.

Number 22 took a swing at him. And missed. Nick backed away, still smiling, with his hands raised, palms forward. The referee stepped in between them and threw 22 out for fighting. Nick, grinning, waved bye-bye to him as he went to the bench.

Nick hit both his foul shots, and, without 22, Alton folded. We won the game by eight points, and when it was over, we charged Nick, all the Owls. I got there first and hugged him and then we all piled on him, hugging him, pounding him on the back.

In our run for the tourney we were two and oh.

CHAPTER 19

IT was late afternoon on Saturday. I was in the town library reading *The New York Times*. I'd never been to New York. But reading the *Times* allowed me to feel like I knew something about a world of excitement I had never seen. I could read box scores for the Yankees and the Giants and the Dodgers. I could read about famous actors in plays I'd never seen, and famous singers and comedians in nightclubs I'd heard about on Manhattan Merry Go Round. I could read about Toots Shore's, and Jack Dempsey's, and the Stork Club, and fights at Madison Square Garden and St. Nicholas arena. I knew what Tammany Hall was. I knew where Billie Holiday was performing, and Duke Ellington. I knew who was at Carnegie Hall. I knew about Greenwich Village.

Joanie came in and sat down at the library table beside me.

"What are you reading?" she said.

"New York Times," I said.

I liked telling her that.

"You ever been to New York?" she said.

"Not yet," I said.

"But you will," she said.

"Sure," I said. "I'm not staying in Edenville the rest of my life."

"You want to move?" she asked.

"No. But even if I stay here to live," I said, "I want to travel and stuff."

"What kind of work do you want to do when you're, you know, a grown-up?" Joanie said.

"I want to be a writer," I said.

"Like for a newspaper or something?"

"No," I said. "I want to write books."

"Books?"

"Yes."

"Wow," Joanie said. "I never heard of anybody wanting to write books."

"Well, now you have," I said. "How about you? What do you want to do?"

"I'm supposed to marry a nice man, live in a nice

house, have enough money, have nice children," she said. "You know?"

"Stay here?"

"I guess so," Joanie said. "I think I'm supposed to go where my husband's job takes us."

"You sound funny about it," I said. "You want to get married?"

"I don't know," she answered. "I don't want to be an old maid."

"No," I said.

"You want to get married?" Joanie said.

"Yes," I said.

"What if you don't?"

I was quiet for a time.

"Maybe," I said, "if you didn't get married, and I didn't get married by the time we were, like, thirty-five, we could go someplace and live together."

"Where?" Joanie said.

"Writers can live anywhere they want," I said.

"If you didn't live here, where would you live?" Joanie said.

"I'd like to live in New York," I said.

"New York City?"

"Yes."

"I'd be afraid to live in New York City," Joanie said.

"Even with me?" I said.

"I wouldn't be scared there with you."

"And I wouldn't have to go to New York," I said.

"Because of me?"

"Sure," I said. "I wouldn't want to make you go some-place you didn't want to go."

Joanie smiled and shook her head.

"You're not like other boys, Bobby," Joanie said.

I was wading pretty deep into waters I didn't know much about.

"Is that good or bad?" I said.

"Good," Joanie said. "I just hope growing up doesn't change you."

"It won't change me," I said. "At least not about you."

"We'll always be friends," she said.

"Forever," I said.

"Yes," Joanie said. "Forever."

CHAPTER 20

I was alone, standing out of the light, near some bushes, in front of Miss Delaney's house when the man came again. He parked his car and got out and walked up to the door and rang the bell. In a minute Miss Delaney let him in and the door closed behind them and everything was quiet.

I felt helpless, like a little kid.

Figure it out. You're smart. Figure it out.

I walked slowly around the house. Maybe there was a way to get in. If I got in, I could hide and maybe listen to them next time the man came to talk with Miss Delaney. Miss Delaney lived upstairs. Old Lady Coughlin lived downstairs. She had some kind of little furry black and white dog with a sharp nose and thin legs. As I walked around the house, the dog started yapping and Old Lady

Coughlin came to the back door and looked out. I stopped stock-still in the shadow of some bushes and she didn't see me, and after a minute she went away. I kept moving around the house, staying in the shadows and behind bushes. In back of the house there were two porches, one above the other, one on the first floor and one on the second. Above the second-floor porch was a window. Probably to the attic.

Back out front, I looked at the man's car and had a thought. No one was on the street. I walked toward the car and looked at the house. I didn't see anyone in the windows. I tried the car door on the passenger side. It was open. Nobody locked up much in Edenville. I opened the door, opened the glove compartment, and took a peek. The car registration was in a small leather wallet in the glove compartment. I took it and closed the glove compartment, closed the door, and ran like hell.

Under a light on the wharf, I opened the registration. His name was Oswald Tupper, and his address was 132 County Road in Searsville, which was the next town north of Edenville. I always carried a pencil stub and a little notebook in case I saw something I needed to write down. I took them out, wrote down the name and address, put them back in my shirt pocket, and threw the wallet with the registration into the water. It floated for a while, bumping with the little waves against the foot of the wharf, and then, as the water soaked in, it sank.

I walked up to the bandstand and sat in the dark with my hands in my pockets and my collar up. Searsville was just up County Road a few miles. I could ride my bike there. Across the harbor I could see the lights from Edenville Neck. I was too far to see anything except the lights. But I liked them. I liked looking at the lights of ordinary people, while I was alone, mysterious, outside, in the night.

There was a big old empty house on Pearl Street, with the windows all boarded up. Last summer the Owls decided it would be a perfect spot for a clubhouse. So I climbed up a telephone pole and jumped to a small second-floor roof, and crawled in an open third-floor window. I had to hang from a rafter and drop into the darkness to get in. Afterward it scared me to think about it. What if they had ripped out all the floors? I would have fallen three stories. But they hadn't, and I landed on a solid floor. The other Owls were impressed.

I went to the first floor and opened the back door from the inside and everyone came in and we hung around in there for a while. But pretty soon we decided it was kind of boring in there and we left and never went back. We really just liked breaking in, I guess.

What was I doing? I was fourteen years old, and I was sneaking around in the night spying on a couple of adults, even though Miss Delaney had made me promise not to. I must have been reading *Dime Detective* too much. I looked around the dark, empty bandstand. It was a school night. Joanie would be home. She wouldn't be coming down here in the dark. What did I think I was going to do? I was going to save Miss Delaney. And how did I think I was going to do it? I didn't know yet. But I knew I was going to do something.

I'd have to figure it out.

CHAPTER 21

WE were trailing against Pinefield by one point with seventeen seconds to go when I got fouled and went to the line for two free throws. I was a good ball-handler, but I was a terrible foul-shooter, and all of us knew it. If I hit them both, we would take the lead. I missed them both and felt like I wanted to crawl in a hole. The Pinefield center, a guy named Lou, got the rebound and fired a pass downcourt to one of his forwards for the insurance basket. Nick intercepted and passed to me, alone downcourt, still near the foul line, wanting to die. I took two dribbles and laid the ball in and we won. Nick had saved me. He and I ran to each other and hugged. The other Owls joined in and we did a kind of little dance in the middle of the court, while Pinefield walked sullenly off.

Afterward we hitchhiked back to Edenville.

Nick said to me, "You still friends with Joanie?"

"Sure," I said. "You?"

"We're still going out," Nick said.

"Anything hot going on?" Russell said.

Nick smiled at him.

"You don't know," he said. "Do you?"

"Bobby don't care," Russell said. "He's in love with Miss Delaney."

"How's that going?" Nick said to me. "You finding anything out?"

"I'm getting there," I said.

"What'd you find out?" Russell asked.

"You don't know, do you?" I said.

"Man!" Russell said. "Nobody tells me anything."

Nick and I looked at each other for a minute. But neither of us said anything.

"You think he's still bothering her?" Billy said.

"Yes," I said.

"You been spying on them?" Russell said.

"I keep an eye out," I said.

"You seen him?" Manny said.

I didn't even know Manny was interested.

"Yes," I said.

"He see you?" Billy said.

"Not yet," I said.

"Whaddya mean 'not yet'?" Russell said.

"Nothing. I just mean he hasn't seen me yet."

"You think he will?" Nick said.

"Maybe," I said. "I mean, you hang around long enough, you may get spotted."

Nick looked at me.

"You got some kind of scheme," he said.

I shrugged.

"You got a plan," Nick said. "Don't you?"

"I'm trying to figure it out," I said.

"You could get into bad trouble," Billy said.

"If I do, you guys can save me," I said.

"Have to," Nick said. "Joanie would kill me if I didn't help you."

"Hell," Russell said. "She'd kill us all."

"I'll let you know," I said.

Nick grinned.

"Owl patrol at the ready," he said.

CHAPTER 22

IT was a mild winter. No snow. The temperatures were usually above freezing. The sun was usually out. It was out on Sunday morning when I got on my bike and road up County Road to Searsville.

Number 132 was a small white one-story building near the road with a few cars parked on the gravel parking lot in front. It looked like some kind of meeting hall. In back there was a house trailer parked next to the hall. The trailer was one of those smooth rounded silver ones, and it looked new. There was a wooden sign by the road that said "Church of America" across the top, and underneath that, "The Rev. Oswald Tupper. Service at 11, Youth Group at 1." It was ten past eleven. I leaned my bike on the sign. My stomach was tight, and I felt like I was out of breath.

I looked at everything for a minute. Then I took in as much air as I could and went into the hall. It was small, with folding chairs to sit on. There were maybe fifteen or twenty people sitting down, and up front, there he was. He had on a dark double-breasted suit and a red tie. He was standing at some kind of lecture stand and behind him on the wall was a large American flag with a big crucifix on it.

I realized I was still holding in the breath I had taken. I let it out as quietly as I could and went and sat on an empty chair in the back. I knew he saw me come in. He had looked right at me. But he didn't seem to recognize me. I was, after all, just some kid he'd chased away from his car once. He smiled when I sat down.

"Latecomers are welcome too," he said.

His voice was very round and official-sounding in the church. It didn't have that scary sound it had had when he told me to get away from his car. I looked down at my knees as if I were praying.

"As I was telling the others," Tupper said with a smile, "'we are face-to-face with both disaster and possibility. The disaster is that the war is over, and the white race lost. Franklin Delano Jewsavelt and the kike conspiracy managed to defeat that struggle for racial purity. But therein lies the possibility. The war is over, all is in flux, and the energies of white America can be focused on the preservation, at least here, in this free country, of the purity of the white race."

Jewsavelt? Kike? What in God's name was he talking about?

"The Communists and the Jews," Tupper went on, "would have us coupling with niggers, and raising a generation of baboons who will do what the Jew commissars tell them."

Niggers? Baboons? What in hell was a Jew commissar?

"That is why," Tupper said, "it's so heartening to see young men here. Young men who have not yet been corrupted, young men who are proud to be American and proud to be white. Young men in whom our future rests, if they will take the opportunity that lies before us. If they will stay true to what they are and what they came from."

I looked around the room. The men were nodding agreement with everything Tupper said. As he continued, I nodded when the men did. There were three or four other kids in the room, sitting beside their fathers. They nodded too, when the adults did.

Tupper went on about this stuff for a long time. It wasn't like he used words I never heard. Lots of people said *nigger* and *kike* in Edenville. I was used to it, although it always made me feel uncomfortable. But you never heard a minister say it in a church, like it was religious.

After the sermon we waited while Tupper went to the front of the church to greet everybody on the way out.

"This your first time here, son?" he said to me as I came out.

"Yes, sir."

"What's your name son?"

"Murphy, sir, Robert Murphy."

"A fine old Irish name," he said with a fake Irish accent. "Would you be Catholic?"

"I guess so," I said.

"Well," he said. "No matter. I hope you'll be joining us in youth group this afternoon."

"I have to go home, sir," I said. "But I hope I can come next week."

"I hope so, Robert," Tupper said. "You're just the kind of lad I'm looking for."

I said, "Yes, sir," and moved on.

As I pedaled home along County Road, I kept glancing back to make sure no one was following me.

CHAPTER 23

"**MY** uncle John was in the war," Joanie said. "My mother's brother. He saw one of those Jewish prison camps."

We were on the bandstand. It was sunny, and pleasant for winter. Joanie was sitting in the sun on one of the bandstand railings. I was walking around the perimeter of the bandstand as we talked.

"Concentration camps," I said. "What did he say about them?"

"He wouldn't talk about them," Joanie said. "Just that they were awful."

"I think they killed Jews there," I said.

"That's what Uncle John says."

There were a lot of veterans around Edenville. Guys who'd been on ships. Guys who'd been waist gunners in B-17s. Guys who'd been in North Africa. Guys who'd been in Italy and Europe and the Pacific. Some of the guys had been wounded. Some of the guys who'd been in the Pacific were still kind of yellowish from some jungle disease they'd got. Philly DeCosta was deaf in one ear from being an artillery gunner. Most of them wore some part of their old uniforms around. Leather flight jackets, pea coats, and a lot of old field jackets with the insignia still on them. I still knew most of the patches the way I knew all of the airplanes. Screaming Eagle for the 101st Airborne; blue and white stripes for the 3rd Division. Corporal's stripes. Captain's bars. I always wanted a field jacket, a real one, worn by a real soldier. But the war was over, and I had missed my chance. Unless there was another one. I felt sort of guilty, and I never said it, but I hoped there'd be another one.

"Do you suppose this man is a Nazi?" Joanie said.

"Hard to figure a Nazi preacher," I said.

"Maybe he isn't really a preacher," Joanie said.

"He says he is. He gave a sermon. People come to listen."

"Still doesn't make him a real minister," she said.

"No."

"Are you going to go back for the youth meeting?"

"I don't know," I said.

"Are you afraid?"

"No."

"I would be," Joanie said. "He sounds awful."

I shrugged.

"Remember we promised never to lie to each other," Joanie said.

"Maybe I'm a little scared," I admitted.

She smiled.

"Maybe," she said.

"But I don't know what good it would do me to go," I said.

"Because you know all you need to know about him?"

"I guess."

"I agree," Joanie said. "What we need is to know what's going on with Miss Delaney."

"Yeah."

"Do you have a plan?"

"I'm figuring," I said.

"If you go to that man's youth meeting ever," Joanie said, "I could go with you."

Wow!

"I think it's only for boys," I said.

"Isn't it always," Joanie said.

EVEN *the small movie theaters in second-level cities were impressive. All of them had big velvet curtains on either side of the big screen. There were gilt-trimmed loge boxes on either side of the theater, just like real theaters where they put on plays in New York. Usually there were two movies, a newsreel, maybe a cartoon, previews of coming attractions, and sometimes a short subject, Robert Benchley or some other person like that. . . . Every week during the war, on Saturday afternoons, unless we were playing basketball, we went to see double-feature westerns at The Art Theater on Purchase Street in New Bedford. These weren't westerns like* Duel in the Sun *with Gregory Peck, or* My Darling Clementine *with Henry Fonda. They were more grown-up movies in which we had little interest. In fact, often we hadn't even heard of them. If we did see them, we thought they were kind of slow. Instead we saw Tom Mix and Rocky Lane; Wild Bill Elliott and Bob Steele; Buck Jones, Sunset Carson, Ken Maynard, Johnny Mack Brown, Hoot Gibson, and Randolph Scott . . . We saw every Tarzan movie starring Johnny Weismuller. We would have died to be Boy. We were saddened as Johnny Weismuller got heavier and heavier. We never doubted that the movies were shot on location. The whole question of sex bothered us a little. If Jane and Tarzan were married, who mar-*

ried them? If they weren't married, then what were they doing living together out there in the jungle? Someone told me that they had actually gotten married at the end of one of the books, but I never found the place, and for us, Tarzan was a figure of the movies. . . . We also went to any Boston Blackie movie we could find. Blackie was played by Chester Morris, who was also on the radio: "Enemy to those who make him an enemy. Friend to those who have no friend." We watched Tom Conway as *The Falcon* and anything Bing Crosby was in: Going My Way, The Bells of St Mary's, and the Road *pictures he made with Bob Hope and Dorothy Lamour, which all of us thought were hilarious. Even with these movies we were not at all sure it was not shot in Rio, or Singapore, or wherever. It was years, even after seeing many real cities, before I could imagine a city as looking different than the back lot city of noir films, and B movie detective stories. It was like movies were more real than the life I was actually living.*

CHAPTER 24

I had to find out what was going on between Tupper and Miss Delaney. The only way I could think of was to listen in on them when they were together. And the only way I could think of to do that was to find a place in Miss Delaney's house where I could get in and hide and listen to them. It had to be a place I could get to easily. I'd have to see him go in and then sneak fast into the listening place.

I spent several winter afternoons looking at the house. Old Lady Coughlin was the town librarian. So when Miss Delaney was in school and Old Lady Coughlin was in the library, there should be nobody at their house. There wasn't. Except weekends. I had to get in to get the lay of the land in there. I couldn't do it on a weekend. I would have to skip school. The entrance to the second floor, where Miss Delaney lived, was separate from the entrance to Old Lady Coughlin's. So the dog wouldn't be a problem. He might yap, but so what.

I went to school on Tuesday morning, made sure Miss Delaney was there, pretended to go to the boy's room, and skipped out the side door with my book bag. The library didn't open until an hour after school started, and Edenville was too small a town for a school-age kid to get away with hanging around on the street. I went up to St. Ignacio's and hung around there. It was like a branch church, and it was always open. But Father Al was only there on Friday, Saturday, and Sunday. I figured if I got caught skipping school to sit in the church, how much trouble could I get in?

I liked it in the empty church. The Mass on Sundays was boring. But when it was empty and I was in there alone, I liked the way the sunlight came through the stained-glass windows. I liked the silence, and the hint of incense, and the statues of the Virgin by the altar. I didn't much like the crucifix above the altar. It seemed kind of gruesome to me. But it was part of the whole church thing.

I was doing bad things . . . skipping school, breaking into Miss Delaney's house, spying on people . . . But I was doing them for a good reason. I was trying to save Miss Delaney. . . . Miss Delaney said she didn't want me to save her. But she needed to be saved from that guy.

Oswald Tupper was creepy. And there was nobody else to help her. . . . Sometimes I wished I hadn't been looking out the window that day when I saw them for the first time. . . . It was kind of fun, though. I wondered what Father Al would say.

When it was time, I went out of the church and walked down past the library. Being outside, walking around on a school day, I felt like I was naked in public. As I went past the library, I could see Old Lady Coughlin at the desk. I went on to her house and walked straight up to Miss Delaney's door like I was supposed to be there. I tried the door. It was locked. I looked in the keyhole. I could see the key inside. I took a newspaper page from my book bag and spread it flat and slipped it under the door. Then I took my jackknife and put it in the keyhole and pushed the key from the hole. I heard it land on the floor inside the door. I put my jackknife away and crouched down and carefully pulled the newspaper out from under the door. There was the key, just like it was supposed to be. I'd read about a guy breaking in by doing that trick in *Black Mask Magazine.* I was thrilled that it worked.

I unlocked Miss Delaney's door and went in. I could feel my heart. I could hear it. The sound filled my head. I was breathing hard. The guy in *Black Mask* hadn't been scared. But I was in Miss Delaney's house. What if I found something awful? What if I got caught? I went up the stairs and into her kitchen. Everything was neat and clean. There was a coffee cup and a saucer with toast crumbs on it in the sink. I went slowly through the house. Downstairs the dog was barking. I looked in her bedroom. I felt embarrassed. But it was just a bedroom. Everybody had them. I thought about her undressing to go to bed. My throat seemed to close. I felt like I couldn't swallow. I looked in the living room and in the dining room. She must have used the dining room table as a desk. There were papers and stuff on it, in neat piles. I didn't touch them. I went back to the kitchen. I went back out the kitchen door to the stairs, and up the stairs to the attic. The attic was unfinished. There was a window at either end. There wasn't any floor, but there were boards laid down that you could walk on. In one corner there were a couple of suitcases and a few cardboard boxes. The rest of the attic was empty. I could still hear the dog barking on the first floor. The space between the rafters was full of insulation, but in several places the insulation was pulled aside and I could see some wires going into a metal box, probably for ceiling lights. I crouched down and put my ear close to one of the boxes. I could hear the dog really well. I stood up and went to the back window. I looked out at the roof of the second-story porch. To the left was one of the big old trees that grew near the house. I nodded to myself. Just like that vacant house we'd snuck into. I tried the window. It was locked. I unlocked it and tried again. It opened easily. I closed it again and left it open just a crack. Then I went back down the stairs and locked the back door and left the key in the lock. I went back up to Miss Delaney's apartment and went down the front stairs and came to the front door, which had one of those locks that locks behind you when you shut it. I had my book bag. I had the piece of newspaper in the book bag. I had my jackknife. I took a breath and opened the front door and went out.

CHAPTER 25

I hid my schoolbag in the boys' room and threw the newspaper away in the trash barrel, then went upstairs to my classroom. I felt so strange. I felt like somebody else. I opened the back door of the classroom silently and slipped in and sat down.

"Bobby?" Miss Delaney said.

"Yes, ma'am," I said.

"Where in heaven's name have you been?"

"Boys' room, Miss Delaney."

She nodded.

"See me after class, please," she said.

When class was over and I went to the front of the room, Miss Delaney said, "Are you feeling all right?"

"I was feeling kind of sick," I said. "But I'm better now."

"Why didn't you tell me where you were?" Miss Delaney said.

"I . . . I was embarrassed," I said.

She smiled.

"Yes," she said. "I can understand that."

"You can?"

"Of course," she said. "Some things are embarrassing."

I nodded.

"But we have rules," Miss Delaney said. "And you can't just disappear for much of the day and I let it go."

I nodded again.

"You'll need to stay after school today," Miss Delaney said. "For an hour."

That wasn't bad.

"Yes, ma'am," I said.

She looked at me for a moment. She had very big eyes. Like Joanie. Except hers were brown and Joanie's were blue.

"No argument?"

"No, ma'am."

"And what is all this *yes ma'am* and *no ma'am* business?" she said. "You are usually quite a bit more mouthy."

"I did something wrong," I said. "I know it. I think the punishment is fair."

She looked at me some more.

"Very mature," she said.

"Thank you."

I was pretty sure she knew I was lying. But she didn't say so.

She just smiled and said, "Now go sit down, and while you're serving your time, please write me a two-page essay on why we have to keep track of the students in our classes."

I went back to my desk, sat down, and got out some lined paper and a pen. I was a good writer. The essay would be easy. I knew that. Miss Delaney knew it too.

I felt bad lying to her, and worse because I thought she knew it. Just like I felt bad about sneaking into her house. I seemed to have to do a lot of bad things to do a good thing. It made me uncomfortable. It was kind of spoiling the adventure. But it wasn't just an adventure—Miss Delaney really needed help. What I needed to do was talk with Joanie.

CHAPTER 26

I went up to the Reverend Tupper's youth group meeting on Sunday afternoon, and slipped into the back row. There were maybe fifteen other kids there. Too few to hide among. The reverend spotted me.

"Bobby Murphy," he said in his mock Irish brogue, "sure and ye be welcome among us, Bucko."

I nodded and tried to look pleased. Actually I was so nervous, I thought I might throw up.

"You are just in time, Bobby, to join us in our opening pledge."

Everyone stood up, so I did too. We stood at attention.

"Until I die . . ." the reverend said.

Everyone said, *Until I die . . .*

"I will serve . . ."

I will serve . . .

"This flag . . ."

This flag . . .

"And the great country it represents . . ."

And the great country it represents . . .

"So help me God."

So help me God.

We all sat down. Reverend Tupper was wearing a tan uniform, kind of like a Boy Scout leader, except instead of a kerchief, he had a black tie. Over the tie he wore some kind of medal hanging on a blue ribbon around his neck. Behind him on the wall was a big American flag with a crucifix. The same one that had been in the house trailer church.

"As always," the reverend said, "we begin by reviewing the truth of our mission. The flag of our country is red, white, and blue: red, for the blood shed in the defense of our way of life; blue is for the true-blue loyalty of those who have defended our way; and white for the color of the founding fathers."

All of us sat silently.

"Those of us who served in the war, including those who won the Medal of Honor"—he touched the medal—"as I did, went to war to keep those colors clean and pure. We trusted this country and we were lied to. We were not preserving those sacred colors. We were fighting to advance the cause of godless Communism. We were fighting to repress white Christians. We were making it more possible for black and yellow hordes to mongrelize the population so that racial purity and Christian virtue could be banished. We were manipulated by Franklin Delano Jewsavelt and international Jewry, who conspired to demonize the German people and advance the cause of godless Bolshevism in the name of victory."

We all sat perfectly still listening. It was unbelievable. I had never heard anyone talk that way. I wasn't exactly sure what he was saying, but it was certainly different than anything anyone else had ever said to me about the country and the war. He used words like *nigger* and *kike*, as if they were perfectly okay words. He talked as if Jews weren't white. He spoke of a yellow invasion from Asia. He spoke of the Communist plan to rule the world by stirring up rebellion in the inferior races. He talked like it would have been better if we had joined the Germans and defeated Russia. I was completely amazed.

"I too was deceived," he said. "I fought in this war, on the wrong side, killing Christians on behalf of Jews and Bolsheviks. I was given a Medal of Honor for it. And I am ashamed. I am ashamed of the medal, and I am ashamed of myself. But it is not yet quite too late. We still have a chance to save our nation and our race. It is you who are our chance. You strong, young white Christian men who can choose fertile, young white Christian women and form the breeding stock for a race of cleanliness and purity."

He stopped and gestured toward us with both hands and bowed slightly and clapped, apparently for us. The boys in the audience began to clap back and pretty soon there was loud applause. I clapped along with the others.

"Together," the reverend said, "we will move forward. Together we may save our race."

More applause.

When it died down, the reverend said, "Next week we will begin systematic instruction, with some guest instructors."

Then he stood at attention and we all stood up at attention and he put his right fist over his heart.

"White and Christian until death," he said.

We all put our right fists over our hearts.

White and Christian until death.

CHAPTER 27

I was walking Joanie home from school. I knew Nick saw us. And I was pretty sure he didn't like it. But I had to talk with her. And I couldn't wait. I felt as if my skin were stretched too tight over the rest of me. I talked all the way to the corner of her street and down, and stopped outside her house and kept talking. Joanie listened and nodded and listened.

Finally she said, "Let's go down to the bandstand, I don't want to go in yet."

I could have kissed her. The thought startled me a little in the middle of my long talk. I could have kissed her. I wanted to kiss her. I had never really kissed a girl before. A few on the cheek at spin the bottle games. But real smoochy kissing, no. I wasn't exactly sure how to go about it. Besides, if I kissed her, it would change everything.

She might get mad. And even if she didn't, she wouldn't be my best friend anymore. She'd be . . . I wasn't sure what she'd be. It made me feel strange.

The bandstand was empty as usual. And the harbor was where it always was, empty in winter, only a few boats at mooring.

"So I don't know if I'm doing the right thing or not," I said. "I have to do so many wrong things to do it."

"You think too much about things," Joanie said.

"You have to," I said. "I mean a man has to. How else can he be a good man?"

"Maybe he just is a good man," Joanie said.

"And I haven't even told you yet about the guy," I said.

"Is he bothering you?"

"In a different way," I said. "Wait'll you hear."

"Finish telling me about what's bothering you so far," Joanie said. "Then we can talk about Oswald whosis."

"Well, so far I've lied and broken my word and skipped school and broken into Miss Delaney's house," I said. "I mean, am I a good guy or a bad guy?"

"You're a good guy, Bobby. You know it and I know it."

"How do I know it?"

"You know," she said. "Sometimes you have to do bad

things to do good things. It's bad to kill. But my uncle John killed people and he's not bad. What he did was good. He had to kill people to defend us. All the soldiers did. During the war it was right to kill. Nazis and Japs."

"But now it wouldn't be," I said.

"That's right. Things change. You know you're trying to do a good thing, because you're a good kid who will grow up to be a good man."

I felt my eyes start to fill. I went and leaned on the railing of the bandstand and looked down at the harbor. I nodded my head for a while. But I couldn't think of anything to say.

Joanie came and patted my shoulder.

Finally I said, "The Reverend Oswald Tupper is some kind of crazy man."

I told her about the youth meeting.

"That was really brave," Joanie said. "To go up there like that alone."

I nodded.

"He talks like that," I said. "And yet he's got a Medal of Honor."

"He says."

"I saw it," I said. "He was wearing it on a ribbon around his neck."

"If it really was one," Joanie said.

"You think he's lying?"

"My uncle John got some kind of medal too," Joanie said. "I don't know what. He never shows it to anyone. He never talks about it, and he never ever wears it."

"You think he stole it?"

"Maybe," Joanie said. "Or maybe he bought it from somebody who needed the money. Or maybe he won it for being a hero. I'm just saying that you don't know yet, just because he wears it and says he won it."

"How are we gonna find out?" I said.

"I'll ask my uncle John," Joanie said.

"Don't tell him about me."

Joanie smiled.

"No," she said. "We're friends. We keep each other's secrets."

"And you think I should sneak in there next time he shows up and listen in."

"Yes."

"I don't know," I said. "I don't know if I dare."

"I'll do it with you," Joanie said.

"You?"

"Me."

"You'd sneak into the house with me and spy on them?"

"Yes," she said.

"You'd have to climb a tree," I said.

"I can climb a tree," Joanie said.

"And you're not scared to?"

"Not as long as we do it together," she said.

"Same with me," I said.

CHAPTER 28

WE were down by three points to the Grange Bay JVs, with ten minutes left. Grange Bay had a center almost as tall as Russell, and he was too good for Russell one on one. He was getting a lot of points. And we decided the only way to deal with him was to go straight at him. Wear him down a little. Maybe get him in foul trouble.

I was the best dribbler on the team, so I did the most of it. He blocked my shot twice, and one of Russell's, when I passed off to him. But he picked up two fouls in the process, and had only one left. Next time down the court, with four minutes left, we were hanging in there. Nick and Billy were hitting outside shots, and Manny was doing his usual work on the rebounds. Bringing the ball up, I faked right, dribbled left. Beat my man and ran hard into the Grange Bay center as he moved over to cut me off. Both of us went down, and as we did, I jabbed him hard in the ribs with the elbow away from the ref.

The ref blew the whistle. The Grange Bay center got up and smacked me hard in the mouth. My upper lip started to bleed. Russell jumped in between us with his hands up and his fists clenched, and I grabbed him around the waist and pulled him back.

"No," I said. "No. We got no subs. We got no subs."

The referee stepped in and called a double foul. Me for charging, my third, the Grange Bay center for fighting. His fifth, so he was ejected. Which didn't really matter because he had already fouled out.

"I'll see you after," the Grange Bay center said. "You little creep."

I still had my arms around Russell's waist.

"You'll see all of us after," Russell said, "freaking sucker puncher."

The coach of Grange Bay came out on the court to get his center.

"Settle down," he said. "I'll be around afterward, too, and if there's any fighting, I'll kick everybody's little ass on my team and yours."

He handed me some wadded tissue.

"Stuff that in your nose," he said. "Then wad some up and stick it under your upper lip."

I did as he told me. He watched.

"You ready to go?" he said.

"Yeah," I said.

He nodded.

"You stayed pretty cool, kid, pretty cool."

Then he nodded at the referee, and play resumed. Since there'd been a double foul, we had to jump ball to decide possession. With their center gone, Russell was six inches taller than anybody else on the floor. He won the tap easily, and moved down in close to the basket. Nick passed him the ball and he turned and put in a layup over some guy too short to guard him. In the remaining four minutes, Russell scored ten points and blocked half their shots, and we won by five.

After the game when we changed and were leaving the building, the Grange Bay coach came and walked beside me.

"You give him the elbow when you went down?" he said.

I shrugged.

"I guess so," I said.

"On purpose?"

"Yeah."

"Worked pretty good, didn't it?" the coach said.

I looked up. He was smiling.

"Pretty good," I said.

CHAPTER 29

JOANIE and I met as soon as it turned dark and stood around in the shadow of the bushes and watched Miss Delaney's house.

"Did Reverend Tupper really say 'breeding stock'?" Joanie said softly.

We stood close together in the darkness. I could smell the shampoo she used.

"He said we should choose fertile, young white Christian women and form the breeding stock for a race of cleanliness and purity."

"Ick," Joanie said.

"Are you clean and pure?" I said.

"I think so," Joanie said.

"Then you might do," I said.

"Moo," she said.

"That what breeding stock says?" I asked.

Joanie nodded.

"Was President Roosevelt really Jewish?" she asked.

"I don't think so," I said.

It was our fourth night standing outside Miss Delaney's house. I didn't mind. It meant I saw Joanie every night.

"Is he saying we should have been allies with Germany?" Joanie said.

"I think so," I said.

"He sounds crazy," Joanie said. "All that stuff about Negroes and Jewish people and people from China. That doesn't make any sense."

"I know," I said.

"And what has all that stuff got to do with Miss Delaney?" Joanie said.

"Maybe we'll find out tonight," I said.

The gray Ford Tudor came slowly down the street and pulled up in front of Miss Delaney's house. The bottom seemed to fall out of my stomach.

"Oh my God," Joanie said.

Were we going to really have to do it?

Reverend Tupper got out of his car and looked casually up and down the street and walked toward Miss Delaney's door. He rang the bell. The door opened and he went in. The door closed. I felt as if there were something stuck in my throat. I tried to say something, but made a hoarse noise. I cleared my throat.

"If we're going to do it, we have to go now," I said.

My voice was very scratchy.

"You scared?" Joanie said.

"Yeah," I said.

"Me too," Joanie said.

"Can we do it?" I said.

"Yes," she said. "We'll do it together."

Staying in the shadows, we went along the hedge and around back to the tree beside the house. "You go first," Joanie said.

I nodded. I was supposed to go first. I was the boy. I was having trouble breathing. I paused and took a big breath, then started up the tree. It had plenty of branches and was easy enough to climb, except that my arms and legs felt uncoordinated. I looked down. Joanie was right behind me. She was right. She could climb a tree as good as I could.

I got level with the roof of the porch, and held on to a branch above me while I stepped over onto the roof. I was wearing sneakers. So was Joanie, and dungarees. Joanie came right behind me, and the two of us crouched down by the attic window and listened. We heard nothing. Old Lady Coughlin's dog didn't bark.

The attic window was still open a crack, the way I'd left it, and I slipped my hands under and eased it up. It went easy enough. Then we waited again and listened. I could hear Joanie's breathing next to me. I could hear my own too. But neither of us heard anything else.

I put my mouth next to Joanie's ear.

"There's boards on the floor," I whispered. "To walk on. Be sure to stay on them."

"Can we see in there?" Joanie whispered.

"There's a window at the other end too," I said. "Once we get in, we should stay still until our eyes adjust. Then I think we can see."

"Okay."

I still felt shaky inside. But there was something about being with Joanie that made me less scared. I wondered why. If we got caught, she couldn't fight Reverend Weirdo any better than I could. But I realized suddenly that I couldn't do this without her. Not with the reverend downstairs. I didn't know why that was. And I couldn't be thinking about that now.

I'll figure it out later.

We stood quietly in the dark and waited until we could see. I was right. There was enough light coming in the front window from the streetlights, and enough light coming in the back window from the moon and stars and whatever, that we could see enough to move around.

I knew there were four rooms below us. Kitchen and dining room in the back. Bedroom and living room in the front. I pointed toward the right front corner of the attic and we went along the boards to the space above the living room like we were walking on a bomb. We stopped above the living room. We could hear people talking. Both of us lay down carefully. There was insulation between the rafters. As carefully as I could, I picked some up and moved it until the back of the ceiling showed. We barely breathed as we lay there . . . and we could hear.

"You have no right to keep a boy from his father," Tupper said.

"And you have no right to take him from his mother," Miss Delaney said.

"He belongs to me," Tupper said. "He belongs moreover to the movement."

"Which is why I won't share him with you," Miss Delaney said. "He belongs to no movement."

"You will bring him up to be a whimpering one-world liberal fool," Tupper said.

"I will not permit him to be turned into one of those pathetic little Nazis in your youth group," Miss Delaney said.

I could hear footsteps. It sounded like Tupper was pacing.

"I want my son," Tupper said kind of thoughtfully.

"We've had this conversation before, Richard . . ." Miss Delaney said.

"Don't call me Richard," Tupper said.

"I don't care if you call yourself Batman," Miss Delaney said. "I married Richard Krauss. How did you turn into Oswald Tupper?"

"There was a war," he said.

"There was," Miss Delaney said. "But it didn't turn everyone into . . . whatever you are."

"There are ways to make you tell me," Tupper said.

"And there are police to be called," Miss Delaney said.

"And I tell them that you are a divorced woman with a child? How long do you keep your job when that gets out?"

"You won't do that," she said. "You're too afraid."

"What am I afraid of?" Tupper said.

"I don't know. But you don't want the police involved any more than I do."

Nobody said anything for a moment. Then footsteps, and then it sounded like he slapped her.

"I will do what I must to keep you from the boy," Miss Delaney said. "You bastard."

We heard what sounded like another slap.

Then Tupper said, "Put that down."

"No," she said. "I will not let you hit me again."

"You haven't the guts," Tupper said, "to stab anyone with that."

"If you try to hit me again," Miss Delaney warned, "I will use it."

"You bitch," Tupper said. "You hid that in here before I came, didn't you."

"You've hit me before," Miss Delaney said.

It was quiet below us for a bit.

Then Tupper said, "Perhaps an anonymous letter to the school board . . ."

"If I have any trouble with the school board or anyone else, I tell everyone about you."

Again it was quiet. Then there were footsteps and we heard her apartment front door open.

Tupper said, "If you ever tell anyone about me, I will kill you. And I will kill them."

Then we heard the door close, and very faintly, his footsteps going down the front stairs.

We stayed where we were, trying not to move at all. Below us we heard Miss Delaney walk across the room. And we heard her turn the key in the front door. Then there was silence, as if she might still be standing at the front door. And then she began to cry. Joanie and I stood up carefully and headed for the window. I was pretty sure she wouldn't hear us.

She was crying really loud.

CHAPTER 30

I was walking Joanie to her house. The Ford Tudor was nowhere in sight.

"Did you hear Miss Delaney say *bastard*?" Joanie asked.

"And he called her a bitch," I said.

We walked past the school. Dark now and perfectly still.

"Do you think she had a knife?" Joanie said.

"That's what it sounded like."

Along Church Street, the lights were on in the windows of houses. People were safely inside reading, listening to the radio, playing bridge.

"You think she was married to Reverend Tupper?" Joanie asked.

"I guess so," I said.

"She's got a baby," Joanie said.

"I know."

"You think they'd fire her if they knew?" she said. "I mean, Mrs. Wood is married."

"She's the only one," I said.

"Mr. Welch is married. He has a little kid."

"That's different," I said. "He's a man."

"So?"

"So women when they get married have their husband to take care of them," I said. "If they work after they're married, it's not fair. They're taking the job from a guy who has to support a family."

Joanie didn't say anything for a time.

Then she said, "I guess so."

"Besides," I continued, "I never heard of a divorced teacher."

"And," Joanie said, "they could say she lied to them when they hired her."

"Right."

Joanie's house was ahead.

"Let's walk a little more," I said.

"Yes."

We turned and walked along Water Street. The smell of the harbor was strong and cold. Ice had started to crust around the edges of the eel pond.

"It's not exactly right that a father can't see his son," I said.

"Would you want Reverend Weirdo for a father?" Joanie asked.

"No."

"He threatened her at the end," Joanie said.

"I know."

"And he hit her at least twice."

"I know."

"I wonder what she knows about him," Joanie said.

"She knows his real name."

"I wonder why she ever married him," Joanie said.

I shook my head.

"I hated hearing her cry," Joanie said.

"Yes," I said. "Me too."

"How are we going to stop him?" Joanie asked. "Make him leave her alone?"

"I don't know," I answered. "We need to figure it out."

CHAPTER 31

IT had started to snow about an hour after school started. The first snow of the winter. I was sitting in the back of the classroom looking out the window at the snow, which was soft and steady. There had been a lot of times when I'd said how I'd figure things out *later*. Now it was *later*. I needed to figure out why I felt safer with Joanie. I needed to figure out a lot about how Joanie made me feel. I had to figure out what to do about Nick and Joanie. But most of all, I needed to figure out what to do to help Miss Delaney. I was only fourteen, I had time for the other stuff. But there might not be too much time left to figure out Miss Delaney and her problem.

At least I had an idea what her problem was. Maybe I felt safe with Joanie because I knew I could be brave for her. Even brave, I couldn't go against a grown man. Some of the older guys, war veterans, would probably have been happy to help. But then Tupper would blab, and Miss Delaney would get in trouble. Maybe I felt brave with Joanie because she was brave. Her hair smelled really nice. I had to focus on Miss Delaney. I couldn't let Joanie keep popping in. I could think about Joanie later, once I'd figured out what to do about Miss Delaney. It was funny, every other girl I thought about sex. I didn't know a lot about it. And I'd never done it. But I thought about it. Except Joanie. With Joanie, I thought about Joanie. How were we going to get Tupper to leave Miss Delaney alone? I wondered why he changed his name. Did he change it before he got the Medal of Honor? Richard Krauss.

Russell reached over and punched me in the ribs.

"Miss Delaney's talking to you, Dumbo," he said.

"Thank you, Russell," Miss Delaney said.

"I'm sorry, Miss Delaney," I said. "I didn't hear you."

"I said the education is going on up here. There's nothing to be learned out the window."

"Yes, ma'am," I said.

"Have you read *Gulliver's Travels*, Bobby?"

"I saw the movie," I said.

Several people in the class snickered. Miss Delaney shook her head.

"The book is better," she said. "Marilyn, have you finished the assignment?"

"Yes, ma'am . . ."

I concentrated on the snow again.

Nick and I hadn't been quite as easy with each other since I started being friendlier with Joanie. He was my friend, but Joanie was too. Even though she was a girl, I liked her better. The snow came straight down, and quiet. It wasn't a blizzard or anything, just the quiet steady downfall of big white flakes. If I helped Miss Delaney, the reverend would hurt her. If I didn't help her, the reverend would hurt her.

The thought that Miss Delaney had been married was kind of odd. She had a kid. That meant she'd had sex. That was almost suffocating to think about. I thought about sex a lot when I thought about Miss Delaney. I never thought about sex when I thought about Joanie. I daydreamed about her. I thought about rescuing her from kidnappers or finding her when she got lost in the mountains and killing a grizzly bear to save her. In my daydream I killed it with a knife. She was very grateful.

I looked at Miss Delaney. I looked at the snow outside. My mind kept jumping around. I had to concentrate. Forget about killing grizzly bears with a hunting knife. I had to concentrate on saving Miss Delaney from Oswald Tupper.

CHAPTER 32

AFTER school Nick asked me to come across the street to the bicycle shed with him so we could stay out of the snow and talk.

"Joanie says she doesn't want to go out with me anymore," he said when we alone in the shed.

I kept my face still.

"How come?" I said.

"She says she's too young to get serious about dating."

I nodded.

"I guess we all are, probably," I said.

"She been dating you?"

"No."

"I asked her out twice last week," Nick said. "And she said she couldn't and then the second time I saw her later, you were walking her home."

"I just ran into her," I said. "And we were talking and I walked to her house with her."

It was funny how words were, I thought. *Walking her home* seemed to mean the same thing as *walking to her house with her*. But it didn't.

"Are you going out with her?" Nick said.

Sometime, way back, the bike shed had probably been some kind of horse stable. It still smelled sort of horsey.

"No," I said. "We're friends."

"She likes you," Nick said.

"I like her," I said. "We've known each other all our lives, you know."

"So have we," Nick said.

"Yes."

"We played ball together since we were little," Nick said.

I nodded.

"I showed you how to shoot a jump shot," Nick said.

"Except you showed me wrong," I said.

"Okay, so it was off the wrong foot. But you were still trying to shoot both hands before me."

I nodded.

"Joanie likes you," I said. "She told me you were cute and nice, and not grabby."

Nick smiled. He looked embarrassed.

"Can you talk to her?" Nick said. "About me?"

"I don't know if it will do any good," I said.

"You could try," Nick said.

"Sure," I told him. "I'll try."

We both were quiet for a time. The snow kept coming steady and quiet. It looked like some kind of white curtain across the open front of the shed.

"Joanie is pretty sure about stuff," I said. "She makes up her mind, it's kind of hard to get her to change it, you know?"

"Do you not want to talk to her about me?" Nick asked.

"No, it's not that," I said. "But I don't know how much good it'll do."

"I know that," Nick said. "And if you don't want to talk to her about it, that's okay."

"I do," I said. "I'll talk to her."

"Because I think you're hot for her too," Nick said.

"We're friends," I said.

"That's crap," Nick said. "You're as hot for her as I am."

I started to say something, but Nick pushed past it.

"And that's okay. You got a right. We're friends. We been friends all our lives. If I don't get her and you do, okay. We're friends, we'll stay friends."

"Nick," I said. "I . . ."

"Forget it." Nick was shaking his head. "I said what I wanted."

He put out his hand. I shook it.

"Owls for all," Nick said, "all for Owls."

And we laughed.

CHAPTER 33

IN the school yard at recess, Joanie was with her girl-friends and I was leaning on the wall with the Owls. She saw me, and waved for me to come over. I walked over. I could feel Nick looking at me. She met me halfway.

"Meet me at the bandstand after school," Joanie said. "I got things to tell you."

"Me too," I said.

She smiled and nodded.

"Want to come back to my friends with me? We're talking about boys."

"That's funny," I said. "We were talking about girls."

Joanie laughed and went back to her friends.

"You say anything to her?" Nick said to me in a half whisper.

"This afternoon," I said.

Nick nodded.

"Who we playing Saturday?" Billy asked.

"Wickford Junior High," Russell said. "They're undefeated."

"So are we," I said.

"So far," Manny added.

The bell rang and we went back in. I could never decide if I hated school most in winter. In winter it was hot in the classroom and everything reeked of the steam heat in the banging iron radiators. The windows were all closed. Your clothes were too warm. The teachers, even Miss Delaney, seemed locked into hell with you and droned on while you thought about other stuff.

Eventually it was over, and I walked down through the clean white landscape to the bandstand. It was pretty now. Most of the snow was still fresh. In a few days it would be ugly. But not yet.

No one had shoveled a path in, so I had to wade through a foot of snow to get there, and had to wipe off a lot of snow to sit on the bench. Joanie came a few minutes after. She was always later because she went home to change into play clothes. She came in through the snow, carefully stepping in the trail I had broken, and sitting on the bench where I had brushed away the snow.

"I went to the library and asked Old Lady Coughlin if there was a list of Medal of Honor winners from the war," Joanie said as soon as she sat down. "I told her I was doing a special project in school. And she said that she didn't think the library had a list, but she was pretty sure *The Standard Times* would have one. And I asked how I could get it, and she told me I could call the research department at the paper. I asked if they would give it to a kid, and Old Lady Coughlin said maybe not, and she would call for me, and she did."

"And they sent you the list?"

"Yes. She called my house last night and told me."

"What?" I said. "Is he there?"

"Yes," Joanie said.

"Oswald Tupper?"

"The medal was awarded to Oswald Tupper . . . posthumously."

"Yeah, but . . ." I stopped. "He's dead?"

"Yes."

"You're sure?" I said.

"That's what it said on the list," Joanie said. "That's what posthumous means."

"And he didn't get it as Richard Krauss?"

"Richard Krauss wasn't on the list," Joanie said.

"So who was Oswald Tupper?" I said.

"And how did the reverend get his medal?" Joanie said.

"And his name?" I said.

A seagull came and landed in the snow a few feet from the bandstand and looked at us, tilting his head one way and then the other. He had eyes like black BBs. The end of his beak had a little hook in it. We looked at him and didn't say anything, and I thought about what Joanie had found out.

"You have any idea what to do now?" I asked.

"No."

"Maybe if we talk about other things . . .," I said.

"Okay," Joanie said.

"I talked with Nick," I said.

"About me?"

"Yes."

"What did he tell you?" Joanie said.

"He said you broke up with him."

"I couldn't *break up* with him," Joanie said. "He was just a cute boy I went to a party with. He was getting too serious."

"That's what he told me," I said.

"Was he mad at me?" Joanie said.

"No. He was a little sad, I guess."

"How about you," Joanie said. "Was he mad at you?"

"No. He said we were friends all our lives and we'd keep on being friends. He was pretty nice about it."

"Yes," Joanie said. "He is nice."

"You and I been friends all our lives too," I said.

"I know."

"You're the only girl I was ever friends with," I said.

"I know," Joanie said. "Why is that, do you think?"

"I guess I'm kind of shy with girls."

"Except me," she said.

The seagull must have decided we weren't going to feed him. He spread his wings quite suddenly and flew off.

"What if I got serious?" I said.

My voice sounded kind of small to me. I didn't look at Joanie. I watched the seagull head out across the harbor.

"We're different," Joanie said.

"But what if I did?" I said.

"Are you getting serious?" Joanie said.

"No."

I stopped watching the seagull and looked at her.

"But what if I did?" I said.

Joanie smiled.

"We'll see what happens when you do."

There was something in her face that made her seem completely grown-up.

CHAPTER 34

WE played a bunch of preppies from the Phillips Country Day School. They were pretty slick. At the end of the first half they were beating us by ten points. They had a center as tall as Russell, and Russell wasn't so good against people his size. Both their guards were better than I was. But they were all sucking air when the first half ended.

"Okay," I said before the second half. "They're probably better than us. But they're in lousy shape. And we're not."

"So we run them," Nick said.

"Every time we get the ball," I said. "Run like hell. We throw the ball away some, we can live with that."

"Defense?" Manny asked.

"Press," I said. "All over the court. We're in shape.

They're not. We give up a couple layups, we can live with that."

"Besides," Billy added, "it's the only chance we got."

"My man can't keep up with me now," Russell said. "By the time the game's over, he'll be puking on the floor."

They won the tip to start the second half, and we surprised them with our press. So much so that one of their guards lost the ball out of bounds. We brought it in from the side and surprised them again. The whole first half we'd brought the ball up at a normal pace, looking to set up our weave, trying to set up some screens, trying to get Russell free of his man on a roll to the basket. This time Manny threw the ball in to me and I went full tilt up the court, running as hard as I could, in only about half control of my dribble. But it worked. I blew by everyone and laid the ball in. Then they took it in from the end line, and we stayed right up there with them. Face-to-face. Fighting them on every pass. Bothering them on every dribble. When we got the ball, all of us ran for their basket like a Chinese fire drill.

Occasionally we did lose the ball. I lost my dribble a couple of times. Nick threw it away once, trying to hit Russell. Manny got a rebound and threw it the length of the court to Billy but overthrew it. On defense sometimes, one of their guys would break past one of us and go in to score.

But as the half moved on, we also began to get layups, and they began to lose the ball more and more. Hurried passes. Double dribbles. Bad shots. Russell was getting to the basket ahead of his man and getting layups. Phillips took all their time-outs, and when they came back, we were right up against them again. We'd played with only five guys the whole season. All of us were tired. But none of us were exhausted. The Phillips guys looked like all they wanted to do was go sit down.

With two minutes left in the game, we were tied and they ran out of gas. We scored the last eight points while they sort of walked up the floor after us. When the buzzer sounded, they all did go right to the bench and sat on it, heads hanging, gasping for breath, too tired even to shake hands or tell us we were just lucky.

We weren't lucky. We were in shape.

CHAPTER 35

I was with Joanie in the bowling alley, sitting in the back row of benches, having a Coke, watching them bowl.

"I went to see Miss Delaney," she said.

"You did?"

"After school," Joanie said. "The day after we found out about that guy Richard Krauss."

"You didn't say anything did you?"

"Nothing bad," she said. "I told her I was starting to think about college."

"College?" I said. "We're in the eighth grade."

Joanie ignored me.

"And she said that was wise, it was never too early."

"Okay," I said.

"So I told her I was wondering where she went," Joanie said.

"Miss Delaney?"

"Yes, and she told me Colby College."

"Where's that?" I said.

"In Maine someplace," Joanie said.

"Who wants to go to college in Maine?" I said.

"And I said did she have a yearbook or something I could look at, and she gave me hers. She brought it in the next day."

"Her college yearbook?" I said.

Joanie reached into her book bag and pulled the yearbook out. It was white. On the cover in blue letters it said "ORACLE," and down lower the year, 1942. We sat together on the leatherette bench in the bowling alley and read it. The student photographs were alphabetical, and there she was, Claudia Delaney. There was a list of things she'd been in, and some phrases that were probably funny if you knew, but didn't mean anything to us.

"She looks the same," I said.

"Yes," Joanie said. "Except her hair's different."

"She would have been what, twenty-one, I guess."

"Now look at this," Joanie said, and turned to the *K* listings. There, between Kantor and Kroll, was Richard Krauss.

"It's Tupper," I said.

"Yes."

"He's from Lynn."

"Yes."

"Where's Miss Delaney from?" I asked.

Joanie flipped back to Miss Delaney's page and said without looking, "Marblehead."

"They must have met in college," I said.

Joanie flipped back to Krauss.

"He played football," she said.

I nodded.

"If they graduated in June 1942," Joanie said, "the war started during their senior year."

"He probably went in the army after he graduated," I said.

"And they probably got married before he went," Joanie said.

"So the kid could be like three years old," I said.

The alley bowled duck pins. Sometimes when I was broke I used to set pins in the alley. Sit on a little shelf behind the pins. Jump down, step on the pedal to raise the spikes. Set the pins on the spikes. Take your foot off the pedal, and jump back up on the shelf. Sometimes some jerk would bowl while you were still setting the pins, but if you kept your foot on the pedal, the ball just ran into the pins and stopped. Sometimes the pins would get bent and they'd have to close the alley, but that wasn't my fault, and it was better than getting a bowling ball in the face.

There were mostly men in the bowling alley. Some

grown-up women. Some guys our age. Not many girls. But Joanie didn't seem to mind. She always seemed comfortable wherever she was.

"So why did he take somebody else's name?" Joanie asked.

"Maybe he did something wrong," I offered. "Maybe he knew the guy who died and he had done something bad, so he pretended to be him instead of who he was."

"How would you do that?" Joanie said.

"I don't know," I said. "It was probably pretty confusing during the war."

"What do you think he did?"

"I don't know," I said. "It would have to be pretty bad."

"How are we going to know?"

"We'll figure it out," I said.

EVERY *Friday night during the school year, we went to danc-ing class in the Grange Hall. It was a big old building with some sort of churchlike tower on it. I wasn't really sure what a grange was, but I knew it had something to do with farmers.*

The class was taught by a single lady named Miss Miller who played music on a piano in the corner, and would count for us as we glomped around the floor.

None of us exactly liked dancing class. But they insisted we go, and it was a chance to hang with your friends and dance close with girls. Miss Miller insisted we dress up for class, so the girls mostly wore big skirts and white socks and loafers. On top they usually had sweaters, sometimes with a little dickey under the sweater, and sometimes they'd wear a blouse, usually white, instead of a sweater. When you danced with them, you could feel the sharp push of their bra against your chest. The bras were very hard.

I usually had on gabardine slacks and a brown plaid jacket, and either a maroon or a green rayon shirt, with the collar open and spread out over the neck and lapels of the jacket. Most of the guys wore the same kind of stuff. Some kids wore sweaters instead of suit coats.

We were also supposed to learn manners from Miss Miller.

She was always saying "Young gentlemen" this, and "Young ladies" that, and acted as if we would want to be young gentlemen and ladies. Most of the guys, I knew, were not much interested in being young gentlemen. Most of us were interested in sex. We didn't think that girls were; we thought they were interested in being young ladies. But we might have been wrong.

The problem with being so interested in sex was that we didn't really know how to express the interest, or what to do about it. Most of us knew the facts of life in a technical sense. We just lacked what you might call hands-on experience. So we made jokes, and talked sort of dirty, and danced as close as we could. And then retreated to our side of the room and huddled among our gender mates.

The Grange Hall had a bad heating system, so it was always too hot or too cold in there. And the real issues of sex and uncertainty that made the air in the Grange Hall thick with intensity was far beneath Miss Miller's plane of vision. She played her piano and counted for us and talked about "young gentlemen" and "young ladies." If Miss Miller had ever thought about sex, she seemed to have stopped a long time ago.

Dancing with Joanie was, of course, the most pressure. Neither of us could dance, and as we bumped around the barnlike room, we giggled a lot. But I also smelled her shampoo, and felt the hard pointy bra against my chest, and felt her thighs move. I almost closed my eyes in the effort not to think impure *things about her. I didn't want to have to tell Father Al I'd had impure thoughts about Joanie Gibson . . . I didn't want to have them, she was too important to think about like that . . . I forced any bad feelings back down into the bottom of my soul . . . Sometimes I said several silent Hail Marys to distract me. They worked. Or it worked. Or something worked. I didn't have impure thoughts about Joanie, but the effort of not having them was so powerful that sometimes it was difficult for me to talk.*

CHAPTER 36

IT was about half past three in the afternoon. School was over for the day. Joanie and I were squeezed into the phone booth outside Romeo's Package Store next to the Village Shop.

"All my uncle John could think of," Joanie said, "was the Veteran's Administration."

The copy of the Medal of Honor list that Old Lady Coughlin got for Joanie said that Oswald Tupper was in the 1st Infantry Division, 26th Infantry Regiment, 3rd Battalion, Company L. Joanie had it written on a piece of paper along with the number for the VA. She dialed the number.

"Hi," she said. "I'm trying to locate my brother."

She held the phone away from her ear a little and I pressed my head against hers to listen.

"He is a veteran of what service?" the VA woman said.

"Excuse me?"

"Army? Navy? What service?" the VA woman said.

There was the kind of impatience in her voice that kids always hear from grown-ups.

"Army," Joanie said.

"And he's missing?"

"Yes, ma'am. He went to war and now it's over and we haven't heard from him and my mom's awful sick . . ." Joanie said.

"I'll transfer you," the VA lady said.

We waited. Another lady picked up. Joanie told her story again. We got transferred again. Finally we got a guy. He sounded like a young guy.

". . . and I don't know how much time my mom has left," Joanie said.

She sounded ready to cry.

"I understand," the young man said. "What is your name?"

"Janie Krauss."

"And your brother's name?"

"Richard. Richard Krauss."

"Do you have any kind of address for him?" the young man asked.

"I don't know. I have an address, but I'm not sure it's his," Joanie said.

"Let's try it," the young man said.

Joanie gave him Oswald Tupper's military address.

"The Big Red One," the young man said. "That would be European Theater."

"Can you look and see?" Joanie said.

"Hang on," the young man said.

It was cold outside, with a lot of wind. But in the small telephone booth, with the door closed, the two of us were perfectly warm. We stayed with our heads together, listening. We didn't want to talk in case the young man came back on the line. So we were silent. It took forever. But finally he was back.

"Janie?" he said.

"Yes, sir."

"That was the correct address for your brother," he said.

"Do you know where he is?" Joanie said.

The young man paused.

"No," he said after a moment. "I don't."

"Can you tell me anything?" Joanie said.

Again the young man paused.

"Please," Joanie said. Her voice was desperate. "Please. I don't have a father. My mom's dying. I don't know where my brother is. Please tell me something. Anything. Please."

"I was with the Forty-fifth Division," the young man said. "At Anzio."

Joanie and I waited.

"I'll lose my job if you tell anyone I told you," he said.

"I'll never tell," Joanie said. "I promise."

"And," the young man said, "there's other jobs, anyway."

"I won't tell," Joanie said.

"I'm sorry," the young man said, "but your brother is listed as a deserter."

"A deserter? Like, you mean AWOL?" Joanie said.

"Sort of like that," the young man said.

"Oh my God," Joanie said.

"If you find him," the young man said, "he needs a lawyer."

"Yes, sir," Joanie said.

CHAPTER 37

IT was too cold for the bandstand, so we went into the Village Shop. We had three nickels left from the phone call, so I went to the jukebox while Joanie ordered two black cows from Alice at the soda fountain. I played an Andy Russell record, one by Eddy Howard, and Johnny Mercer singing "Personality" with the Pied Pipers.

We took our black cows to the far back booth and sat down.

"Wow," I said. "You were like Barbara Stanwyck or somebody."

"I know," Joanie said. "I thought I might actually cry at one point."

I'm laughing on the outside, crying on the inside, 'cause I'm still in love with you.

"I love Andy Russell," Joanie said.

"I know," I said. "Girls do. That's why I played him."

"The guy at the VA was nice," Joanie said.

"Yes," I said. "I played Eddy Howard too."

"Oh good," Joanie said, "which one?"

" 'To Each His Own'."

"He does that great," Joanie said.

We listened to Andy Russell for a moment

Friends see me out dancing, carefree and romancing . . .

"How bad is it to be a deserter?" Joanie said. "Isn't that pretty bad?"

"I think they can get the death penalty," I said.

Joanie widened her eyes and pursed her lips and blew out her breath.

"Yowch," she said.

"So you can see why Krauss would want to be somebody else."

"You think that's what happened?"

"He was in the same outfit that Oswald Tupper was. I say he deserted. Knew about Tupper dying and getting a medal. So he took his name."

"Wouldn't he have been smarter?" Joanie said. "Not to take a guy who won the Medal of Honor? I mean, other guys must have gotten killed too, that no one would ever hear of."

"Maybe Tupper hadn't gotten the medal," I said,

"when Richard Krauss took his identity. Maybe Krauss is a little crazy. You heard him talking to Miss Delaney."

I ate some of the ice cream out of my black cow with the long spoon that came with it. The Andy Russell song was over. Eddy Howard was on.

. . . or its lovely promise won't come true , . . .

"Do you think they'd actually execute him?" Joanie said.

"They'd do something," I said.

"God," Joanie said. "If we turned him in and they executed him . . . wouldn't you feel weird about that?"

"I don't think we're going to turn him in," I said.

"So what are we going to do?"

To each his own, I've found my own. And my own is you . . .

"I don't think we have to turn him in," I said. "If he knows we know, maybe he'll leave Miss Delaney alone."

"Or we'll turn him in?" Joanie asked.

"I guess so," I answered.

"It's like we'd blackmail him," Joanie said.

"Maybe," I said.

"But what if he . . . did something to us."

"We'd have to be careful," I said.

"If a bunch of people knew . . . ," Joanie said.

"He couldn't do something to all of us," I said.

The third record came up on the jukebox.

When Madame Pompadour was on a ballroom floor . . .

"But we promised Miss Delaney we wouldn't tell anyone."

"Actually," I said, "I promised, and then I told you."

"Telling me is different," Joanie said.

Said all the gentlemen "Obviously, the madam has the cutest personality."

"Because?"

"Because we're best friends," Joanie said. "We tell each other everything."

I nodded.

And when Salome danced and had the boys entranced . . .

"But she'll know what we've done," Joanie said. "Maybe she won't like it."

"We gotta tell her," I said.

"Together?" Joanie said.

"If you don't want to," I said, "I can do it alone."

Joanie nodded and put her hand out suddenly and rested it on my forearm. She smiled, and I felt as if I might start on fire or something.

"We'll do it together," she said.

What did Romeo see in Juliet?

Or Pierrot in Pierrette?

Or Jupiter in Juno?

You know!

CHAPTER 38

IT was snowing again. We stayed after class until everyone else had gone, and then I said, "Miss Delaney, can we see you?"

"Of course," she said. "Come down front."

I got up and went and closed the classroom door. Miss Delaney smiled.

"Are we going to have a confession?" she said.

Joanie and I sat at the two desks in front of Miss Delaney. Outside the windows, the snow was different than the last snow. The flakes were small, and the wind was blowing the snow around. I looked at Joanie. Then at Miss Delaney. I took in a big breath.

"We know about Mr. Tupper," I said.

Miss Delaney didn't move. Her expression didn't seem to change, but somehow her face got sort of sharp and hard, and she looked kind of pale.

"What do you know about Mr. Tupper?" she said.

I felt very small and stiff. I felt like if I moved quick, I might break.

"We know he was married to you. We know about your son."

Miss Delaney's voice was as flat as the top of her desk.

"*We* is you and Joanie?" she said.

"Yes, ma'am."

"Anyone else?"

I shrugged.

"Mr. Tupper," I said.

"Besides him."

"No."

Joanie was completely still at the next desk. I wanted to reach out and touch her. But I didn't.

"I thought we had a promise," Miss Delaney said.

"We had to break the promise," I said. "So we could help you."

"You and Joanie?"

"Yes, ma'am."

Miss Delaney leaned back in her chair and the sharpness kind of went away. She put her hands over her face for a minute. And rubbed her eyes. Then she took her hands away and rested them on her desk.

"What have you done to help me?" she said finally.

"I . . . we . . . we know Mr. Tupper is really Mr. Krauss."

She nodded silently. She seemed tired, like too tired to fight about it, like she had given up.

"We know Mr. Krauss is a deserter," I said.

Miss Delaney stopped nodding.

"What?"

"The army wants him as a deserter," I said. "Did you know that?"

"No," she said. "I didn't. I never knew why he took another name."

"Oswald Tupper really did win a Medal of Honor," I said. "But he got killed in the war. He and Mr. Strauss were in the same place in the army."

"And Richard took his name," Miss Delaney said.

The snow outside was getting blown all around, so that sometimes it was going sideways, and sometimes it even looked like it was going up.

"Have you talked to anyone else about this?" Miss Delaney said. "Anyone?"

I wanted to lie.

"I told the Owls a little about it," I said. "They're ready to help."

Miss Delaney stared out at the snow blowing around outside the second-floor window. Then she looked up at the ceiling.

"My gang," she said.

"They won't tell," I said.

Miss Delaney nodded. She seemed very sad.

"What do you think of all this, Joanie?" she asked.

"I think Bobby was right to try to help."

Miss Delaney nodded again.

"If he weren't a fourteen-year-old boy," she said.

"He's very smart," Joanie said.

Miss Delaney put her elbows on the desk and her fingertips together and rested her fingertips on her chin. She tapped her chin gently and didn't say anything. Then she took a big breath and blew it out.

"I met Richard in college," Miss Delaney said.

"Yes, ma'am," I said. "Colby College."

She looked at Joanie.

"That's why you wanted my yearbook."

Joanie nodded.

"He was a hero in college," Miss Delaney said. "Football star, very handsome, good student. The other boys looked up to him. Girls all wanted to date him."

Joanie and I were very quiet.

"We began dating in our junior year, and we got married the day after graduation. Three months later I was pregnant and he was in the army, overseas. My son was born June 5, 1943. His name is John Strauss. I lived with my parents during that time. Richard was in Italy then, and we wrote each other often, and I sent pictures of Johnny. After Italy he went to England, and in 1944, he was in the Normandy invasion. And then one day he wrote me a letter saying *good-bye*. No explanation. Just *good-bye for a while*. He hoped he'd see me again. I wrote back. But I never got an answer. I wrote the War Department and never got an answer. My parents didn't have much money. My father couldn't support us forever. I had a baby. I didn't know what had happened to my husband. I started looking for a teaching job. I didn't want to tell them about the baby, for fear they wouldn't hire me. I didn't know what to tell them about my husband. So I pretended to be single, and I used my maiden name."

It had started to get dark outside, the way it does in the winter before the afternoon is even over. It was as if we were closed up in this little lighted classroom, and the only people in the world were Miss Delaney and Joanie and me, surrounded by snow and darkness forever.

"In January 1945," Miss Delaney said, "I got the job here, starting in September. And a month later my husband showed up. It was as if I didn't know him. He had a new name. He was angry. He wanted a divorce. And he wanted custody of the child."

Miss Delaney shook her head.

"He didn't even know Johnny. He'd never seen him before. I asked him what had happened. He said I wouldn't understand. It was the war, he said. If you hadn't been in the war, you couldn't understand. He barely looked at Johnny when he met him. He just wanted custody. Like of an object. Like *I want that lamp.*"

She sat thinking about it.

"So you got divorced?" Joanie said.

"Yes. But no custody. He said it didn't matter. He would take the child anyway. I couldn't take this job and take care of Johnny too. My father took a job in another city. Not much of a job. My father is a laborer and spent everything he had to get me through college. They moved there and took Johnny, so Richard couldn't find him. I send them money every month. It's why I need this job."

Miss Delaney smiled kind of sad.

"Johnny has been with them since he was born," she said. "He's comfortable with them. I probably miss him more than he misses me."

"And you took this job," I said.

"Yes, as soon as my parents left with Johnny. A month later Richard moved to the next town and started his church of whatever. And began badgering me about Johnny."

"He hit you," I said.

"Yes," Miss Delaney said. "He has threatened to kill me. But he doesn't know where the child is, and I don't think he would kill me unless he did."

"Then he would?" Joanie said.

Miss Delaney shook her head.

"I don't know," she said. "I don't know him. Whatever happened in the war, he's no one I ever knew. He seems crazy."

"And you couldn't tell the police," Joanie said.

"Tell them what?" Miss Delaney said. "That he hit me or threatened me? I can't prove it. Just my word against his."

"How about how he changed his name?" I said.

"Oh, I suppose," Miss Delaney said. "But everyone would find out about me in the process. A divorced woman with a child, who lied to get this job?"

We all sat quietly for a time. It was like Miss Delaney had said everything.

Finally, I said, "What are we going to do?"

"I don't know," Miss Delaney said. "Do you?"

"I think so," I said.

CHAPTER 39

IT was Saturday. We had our final game of the regular season against a junior high school team from Fall River. Our record was fourteen and oh. So was theirs. One of us would go on to be in the state tourney. Changing in the high school locker room I was so nervous, my stomach was rolling. These guys were good. They were part of a feeder program for Durfee High, which was a basketball powerhouse in the whole state, not just eastern Mass.

Warming up before the game I felt stiff and awkward. The ball felt heavy. We were all nervous. Even Manny looked a little pale. Russell kept swallowing, his Adam's apple moving every time he did. Their coach was one of the high school assistants, and the Durfee coach himself had come to watch. He was so famous, I recognized him from his picture. The Fall River guys gathered around their coach before the tip-off and he talked to them. The five of us kind of stood together, but none of us knew what to say really. If we won, we were in the tourney. And all of us were so tight that it was hard to talk.

There were even a few spectators. We never had spectators. I glanced up at them. *Joanie!* It felt like I'd stuck my finger in a light socket. She was there, sitting by herself in the first row. Big tan skirt, pink sweater, a small round white collar showing. She saw me see her and she smiled and waved. I nodded.

Usually when a game starts the nervousness goes away and you are playing. This time it didn't. We threw the ball away. We missed layups. I lost my dribble twice. The guy from Fall River just took it away from me. Russell was taller than their center, but the Fall River center was heavier and was pushing Russell around like Russell was made of straw. Billy was missing badly from the outside, Nick lost the ball when he drove to the basket, and, at least twice, put up air balls while trying to shoot a layup. Only Manny seemed normal. He did what he does. He rebounded. He put back some of the rebounds for layups. He set screens for Billy and Nick. He kept his man from scoring. He dropped off his own guy sometimes to help Russell with the Fall River center.

Fall River must have been more nervous than they looked, because at halftime they were only five points ahead of us. They should have been up thirty. In the locker room we sat around looking at each other.

"We're blowing this," Nick said.

Russell was unusually quiet. He still looked pale, as if he had stomach flu or something.

"You see Joanie Gibson is here?" Billy said.

"She brought four friends," Nick said. "They could probably beat us."

"We got another half," Manny said.

Everyone was quiet. All of them looked at me. What the hell was I supposed to do? Win one for the Gipper? I thought about Joanie. I thought about Miss Delaney. All of them kept looking at me. We had a half a game to make it or break it. *Win one for the Gipper.*

"They're not that good," I said.

"Better than us," Nick said.

"But they're not," I said. "We're just playing awful."

"Awful," Billy agreed.

"Because we're choking," I said. "Because this is the biggest thing we've ever had happen to us."

"You're nervous too," Russell said.

"Yeah," I said. "I am. But we're thinking about this wrong. This is a big deal to us because we're all fourteen years old, and we don't know much."

They didn't like what I was saying, but nobody had much to say about it.

"Lemme tell you about somebody who has a real problem," I said. "Not some basketball game."

"It gonna help me make a layup?" Nick said.

"Might help you relax a little," I said. "You know I told you about a guy bothering Miss Delaney?"

"Yeah," Nick said.

"Here's the story," I said, and told them everything I knew about Miss Delaney and Richard Krauss, and Oswald Tupper and Miss Delaney's little kid. At first they looked a little annoyed, and then they looked interested, and then they began to look mad.

"He might kill her?" Billy said.

I shrugged.

"She thinks he could," I said.

"God," Manny said.

"We gotta do something," Russell said.

"We will," I said. "After we beat the ass off these guys in the second half, I'll tell you what we're going to do about Miss Delaney."

"Joanie's been in this with you," Nick said.

"Yes."

Nick nodded.

"You see her in the stands?" Nick said.

"Yes."

It was time for the second half. I walked to the locker room door. I grinned at the other Owls and opened the door.

"Let's go, girls," I said.

"Screw you and Knute Rockne," Russell said as he went out to the court. But he didn't look so pale anymore.

As the second half developed, Russell stopped trying to push back against their center and was now rolling off him and cutting for the basket. Nick sank two outside shots behind Manny's screen, and when his man started playing up on him, Nick would dribble past him for a layup. He even hit one layup left-handed. Looseness was contagious. By the middle of the fourth quarter we were ahead by twelve points, loose and happy, and having fun. Fall River didn't know what to do with us. We won by fifteen points.

In the locker room afterward we kept walking around saying how we'd won, saying how we were going to the tournament, saying how good we were. Then Russell stood up on one of the benches.

"Okay, we won!" he yelled. "We're good. We're going to the tourney. Now, what are we gonna do about Miss Delaney?"

"Lemme tell you," I said.

CHAPTER 40

IT was March. There were still patches of snow, but it got warm sooner on the south coast than anywhere else in Massachusetts. It wasn't being south so much; we were only about forty miles below Boston. I was told it was because of the Gulf Stream. Whatever it was, it was warm enough again to sit in the bandstand, which was where Joanie and I were sitting. Some boats had gone back in the harbor already, bobbing pleasantly at their moorings. And some little kids were catching blowfish at the end of the wharf.

"When does the tournament start?" Joanie said.

"Next week," I said. "Runs until spring vacation week."

"You were so much better in the last part of the game than you were at first," Joanie said.

"I gave them a pep talk," I said.

"A pep talk?"

"Yeah," I said. "Like Knute Rockne."

"Who's Newt Rockne?" Joanie said.

I shook my head.

"Doesn't matter," I said. "Thing is, I got the idea from seeing you."

"Me?"

"Yes," I said. "I told them about Miss Delaney."

"Everything?"

"Yes."

"Why on earth," she said, "did you do that?"

"We were too tight," I said. "Scared. I thought maybe if they saw how much less important this game was than a lot of things, we might relax. Give us something else to think about."

"And it worked," Joanie said.

"Something worked," I said. "We're going to the state tourney."

"That's wonderful," Joanie said. "You're so smart, Bobby."

"Yes," I said. "So are you. Let's talk about the plan."

"To save Miss Delaney?"

"Yeah."

"The Owls are in?"

"All the way," I said. "They can't wait."

"Miss Delaney says we shouldn't do this, you know."

"I know."

"She says it might be dangerous."

"There's five of us," I said.

"Six," Joanie said.

"Oh, yeah, of course. I just . . . you're a girl, you know?"

"And I can run as fast as you can," she said.

"I know you can," I said.

In fact, I thought she could probably run faster, but I didn't like to admit that.

"It's just that you don't think about a girl doing something dangerous," I said.

"I can help," Joanie said. "I'm in too."

"Okay."

"Miss Delaney says she can't allow us to do this," Joanie said. "It's dangerous and probably illegal."

"She can't stop us," I said. "And we're the only hope she's got."

"We could tell Mr. Welch," Joanie said.

I shook my head.

"He may be an okay guy," I said. "But he's the damn school principal. She's gonna get fired."

Joanie nodded.

"I agree," she said.

"So it's us or she's got no way out," I said.

"I guess it's us," Joanie said.

CHAPTER 41

ON Sunday afternoon, with the sun out and the melting snow making the highway shiny wet, I rode my bicycle up to Searsville and went to Reverend Tupper's youth group meeting.

He had on his tan uniform. He greeted each of us by name. He seemed so pleasant when he did it, it was hard to remember the Richard Krauss we had heard in Miss Delaney's house. Maybe it was just because I knew about Richard Krauss, but as he said hello to everybody, I thought of a casket salesman who had come to our house when my grandmother died. The salesman was all condolences and niceness, and like dead inside. I knew that inside of Reverend Tupper was Richard Krauss.

"Is there anyone in the room," Reverend Tupper said

when we were all settled in, "who doesn't know the facts of life?"

A kid in front said, "You mean sex?"

"Don't speak out, Tommy," Tupper said. "Raise your hand. When called on, stand up and speak directly. It is appropriate to call adults *sir*."

From his seat, the kid said, "Yes, sir."

Tupper stared silently at him, and I thought I saw Richard Krauss peeking out. The kid looked confused, a guy next to him whispered, "Stand up." And he did, quickly.

"Better," Tupper said. "Repeat your question."

"Sir," the kid said, "when you say 'facts of life,' do you mean sex, sir?"

Reverend Tupper was now very sweet.

"Yes, Tommy," he said, " I do."

"Thank you, sir," Tommy said.

"Do you know the facts, Tommy?" the reverend said.

"Yessir."

"Everyone?"

He raised his hand, all of us raised ours.

"Anyone who doesn't?" the reverend asked.

He raised his hand again. Nobody raised theirs. There were kids in there who were sixteen years old. Everybody knew.

"Good," he said. "Today the subject for discussion is

the movie *The Outlaw,* starring Jane Russell. Has anyone seen it?"

He raised his hand. None of us raised ours. Russell had gone with Billy to see it, when it came to the local theater, but they couldn't get in. Nobody would sell them a ticket. Russell blamed Billy. Because he was tall, he thought he looked older, and he claimed it was because Billy had such a baby face.

"Good," the reverend said. "It is a disgrace. It corrupts the great story of America, the conquest of the west, where men stood alone motivated by honor and the spirit of independence to bring law and order to an uncivilized wasteland."

I wanted to see the movie because of the ads showing Jane Russell in a blouse with a very low neck.

"Since the Jews took over our country, morality has plummeted, and *The Outlaw* is a perfect example of a movie that the Jews have promoted to distract us from their plans to slowly turn us over to the Communists."

I wasn't entirely sure what Communism was. I knew it had something to do with our Russian allies, but I didn't know what it had to do with the Jews. I also couldn't think of anybody in the government with a Jewish name. President Truman wasn't Jewish, certainly. Neither was Senator Saltonstall.

"Each of you boys is a defiance of that attempt. Each of you contains the clean white blood of your ancestors. Each of you worships the one true God. You must not defile yourself. You must never succumb to the wiles of someone not of your heritage. To finally repel the Jews, we need an uncompromised line of white Christian men, generations of them, staying strong, keeping the faith."

He churned on like that, getting kind of worked up, shaking his fist, stomping around up in front of his flag. *What a jerk.* Everybody sat and listened. I wondered if anybody took him seriously. They must have. Why would they come if they didn't?

After the reverend was through, we all stood and said our pledge about being white and Christian, and we put our fists over our hearts, and that was it. Reverend Tupper went to the front door to shake each of our hands good-bye. I hung around so that I was the last.

"Before I go," I said. "I have a message for you."

"Really?" Reverend Tupper said.

"From my eighth grade teacher," I said. "You know her. Miss Delaney?"

Reverend Tupper stared at me. He didn't seem so pleasant.

Finally he said, "Give me the message, please."

"Sure," I said. "She wants to meet you tonight, seven

o'clock, at the bandstand in Edenville, down by the wharf. Do you really know her, sir?"

"Is there anything else?" Reverend Tupper said.

"That's all she said, sir."

He nodded and turned back into the meeting hall.

"You gonna meet her?" I said. "Sir?"

He didn't look back, he just walked into the hall and shut the door.

CHAPTER 42

I stood behind some trash barrels, in the shadows behind the package store. I heard his footsteps before I saw him as he came down the little walkway between the package store and the Village Shop toward the bandstand. He paused when he saw her on the bandstand, sitting on the rail, her head turned, looking at the harbor. She was wearing a camel's hair coat with a dark scarf on her head. As he passed me, I came out from the shadows and walked very quietly behind him. The moon was out and nearly full. You could see pretty well, but everything looked sort of pale. It was kind of chilly. But there was no wind.

When he reached the bandstand, he said, "Claudia?"

She turned.

"You're not Claudia," he said.

"My name's Joanie Gibson," she said.

"What are you doing here?" Tupper said.

His voice was getting that sound again.

"Waiting for you," Joanie said.

"Where's Miss Delaney?" Tupper asked.

"She doesn't know anything about this."

Tupper stood motionless at the edge of the bandstand, with one foot on the step. I was ten feet behind him, but he didn't know it.

"Young lady," Tupper said with the jagged edge sound in his voice. "You will tell me right now what you are up to."

He stepped up onto the bandstand. Joanie swung her legs over the rail and jumped down outside the bandstand.

"If I have to chase you, young lady, you will be very sorry."

"You can't catch me," Joanie said.

Behind him I said, "Your name isn't Oswald Tupper."

He whirled toward me, standing now in the middle of the bandstand.

"Your name is Richard Krauss," I said.

He stared.

"Bobby?" he said.

"And you're a deserter," I said.

"Am I?" he said.

His voice seemed very calm all of a sudden.

"We know all about you," I said.

"You're a good kid, Bobby," Tupper said. "And I'm sure that's true of your little girlfriend. But you've got it all wrong."

"No, we don't," Joanie said. "And I'm not his girlfriend."

"Look," Tupper said. "Let's all sit down on one of these benches and I'll explain it to you."

Neither of us moved.

"You owe me a chance to explain," he said.

I walked closer to the bandstand, but didn't go up on it.

"Go ahead," I said.

"It's a mistake that has been made before. There was a man named Richard Krauss in my outfit, and he was killed. I went to him when he fell, and saw that he was dead, and that he wore no dog tags. I wanted him to have an identity, so I put mine on him, planning to correct the matter when there was a lull in the battle. But somehow, in the heat of battle . . ."

He seemed to be lost in the memory of it, walking slowly around on the bandstand. He seemed sweet and sorrowful at what had happened. The way he had seemed jolly and kind when he'd first welcomed me to his youth group.

"They thought I had died and he had deserted."

"You're Krauss," I said. "We've seen your picture in your college yearbook."

He stopped walking for a minute and looked at me. Then at Joanie. He was closer than I thought, and he was very quick. He reached out all of a sudden with his left hand and got hold of my jacket and dragged me toward him onto the bandstand. With his right hand he took a big jackknife out of his pocket and pressed something, and the blade popped open. I felt like I might pass out. At the same time, the little part of me who always sat and watched was thinking, This is real fear, this is what people must have felt in the war. It was the kind of fear that made you sick. I would always remember it.

"I'll tell," Joanie said from off the bandstand. "I'll tell the police and everybody else."

"You come up here now, young lady, or I'll cut your boyfriend's head off."

Russell came out suddenly from behind the corner of the Village Shop.

"I know too," he said.

Tupper seemed shocked. He looked kind of wildly at Russell. I bit his hand where he was holding the knife and stomped as hard as I could on his toes. He dropped the knife and kind of gasped and I pulled loose and jumped off the bandstand.

Tupper picked up the knife.

"I'll kill all of you if I have to," Tupper said.

His hand was bleeding a little where I bit it. His voice sounded funny. Higher than it had been.

"Me too?" Nick said.

He had been behind the wharf office shed, and now he was in full view in the moonlight walking up toward the bandstand. Tupper was holding his big knife low in front of him, moving it back and forth toward us. When he heard Nick, he pivoted in that direction and waved the knife at him.

"How about me?" Billy said.

He came out from behind the other side of the wharf office.

"Or me?" Manny said in his soft voice.

He had been behind some low evergreen shrubs.

"You can't kill us all," I said.

"I can," Tupper said.

He lunged off the bandstand toward me. I ran. He couldn't catch me, so he whirled and dashed toward Joanie. She ran, faster than I had. He couldn't catch her. He stopped and looked around.

"Nigger," he said to Manny and lunged at him.

Manny was the fastest runner of any of the Owls. He got away from Tupper easily. I thought about a story I had read in *Argosy* where they were hunting a bear with dogs. The dogs were all around the bear and every time the bear charged, the dogs in front of him would run off and the dogs behind him would nip at him.

"You can't catch us," I said. "So you gotta do what we say or we tell everyone."

I wasn't as scared anymore. My heart was still beating very hard. But I didn't feel so sick to my stomach now. In the moonlight everything looked pale. But I thought that Tupper looked paler than the rest of us. And even though it was kind of chilly, there was sweat on his face. He backed up onto the bandstand again.

"If any of you tell anyone," he said, "I will find you alone, and kill you."

"No," I said. "You won't."

He stood still on the bandstand, as if he didn't know where else to go. Even though he wasn't moving, he seemed somehow in a frenzy.

"Because all the rest of us will tell on you," I said. "I looked in the encyclopedia in the library. The punishment for people who desert in wartime is death."

"There's been a mistake," he said. "I tried to explain that to you."

"And then you threatened to kill us," I said.

"I was frantic," he said. "I didn't mean it."

"We'll make a deal with you," I said.

"What?" he asked.

"You leave Miss Delaney alone," I said. "And her kid."

"It's my child too," he said.

"You leave both of them alone," I said. "And you move away from here. We don't care where, but it has to be a long way from here, and you never come back and you never bother Miss Delaney again."

It was quiet. I could hear my own breathing. And my heartbeat. He stood alone on the bandstand. The six of us stood around the bandstand. Nobody moved.

"And if I don't?" he said.

"We start talking, including how you threatened to kill us."

"And if I talk about Miss Delaney and the marriage and divorce she didn't mention and the child she lied about . . .?"

"Maybe she gets fired," Joanie said from behind him. "But you get taken away by the army and executed."

"Are you willing to make that swap?" I said.

He looked around at us. He looked at the big knife he was holding. Then he pushed the button and closed the knife and put it in his pocket.

"I accept your offer," he said.

CHAPTER 43

NONE of us knew what to do next. Including Tupper . . . or Krauss. I couldn't figure out what to call him in my head. Tupper, I decided, that's what his name was to me. We stood still where we were, like sometime had stopped the movie projector and a single frame stood motionless on the screen.

"Does Claudia know?" he asked all of a sudden.

"She doesn't know about this meeting," I said.

"Does she know I deserted?" he said.

"Yes."

He put his hands behind his back and began to walk slowly around the bandstand.

"You're children," he said. "You can't know."

He kept walking. It was more like he was talking to himself than to us.

"Every day wondering if you'll die. Every night afraid to go to sleep because you might not wake up. Every day people dying near you."

He stopped and looked toward the harbor, and stood there.

"I had to go," he said to himself, or us, or the harbor, or something.

All of us stood there watching him, none of us saying anything.

"You gotta be gone from here by Wednesday," I said. "Or we tell everybody."

I hadn't really thought about when he would leave. In my head it was like, we face him down, and he disappears. But I didn't know what else to say, and the Wednesday deadline just sort of came out.

"Two days," he said sadly. "Two days for a man who was nearly killed defending a country that has long since gone to hell. Two days."

He shook his head, still looking toward the harbor.

"Risk your life defending the Jews and the coons," he said.

I didn't like him saying the coon stuff in front of Manny.

Tupper turned from the harbor and looked at us; it was a funny look. He looked right at us, but I don't know if he actually saw us.

"You know," he said, "all the movies you see are made by the Jews. You know that they have signed a nigger to play baseball with white men."

We were all starting to shift around a little. We were getting sick of him.

"You gotta be gone by Wednesday," I said to him. "And never come back."

"It wasn't cowardice," Tupper said.

With his hands behind his back, he started walking around the bandstand again.

"It was a revelation. Suddenly, in the midst of the carnage, I realized I could no longer fight this evil war. I was willing to pay any price, take any risk, but not for the niggers and the Jews and the Communists. I would walk away. I would risk the wrath of the army and the disdain of my countrymen, if I had to . . ."

"Probably why he grabbed some other guy's name," Russell said.

"And his medal," Nick said.

Tupper appeared not to hear them.

"But I would not continue in this monstrous betrayal."

Russell walked over to Manny.

"Guy's a lunatic," he said to Manny. "Let's get out of here."

Manny nodded and the two of them walked away.

"We should have been fighting the Communists," Tupper said.

Billy saw Russell and Manny leaving and looked at me. I shrugged. He went after them.

"I don't want to listen to this anymore either," Nick said.

"Me either," I said.

We both looked at Joanie

"Or me," Joanie said.

"The Nazis understood the threat," Tupper said.

He was looking down at the floor as he walked, hands clasped behind his back, like he was musing out loud.

"Wednesday," I said.

And Nick and I walked away with Joanie between us.

"Don't you see?" Tupper said. "Don't you sense it, the poison, the corruption seeping into every small crevice? I did the only thing I could do . . ."

We walked Joanie home, then Nick and I walked partway home together, and separated when Nick went up toward his house and I kept on toward mine. As soon as Nick was out of sight, I started running toward home.

He never said, and neither did I. But I'll bet Nick did the same thing.

CHAPTER 44

ALL day Monday and Tuesday I walked around with a sinking feeling in the middle of my stomach, like you get sometimes going down in an elevator. In class, I thought Miss Delaney seemed a little tired, but maybe it was just me. Nobody else seemed to notice.

On Wednesday after school, all of us, Joanie too, rode our bicycles up to Searsville. We stopped and huddled up just before we got there, at a bend in the road, out of sight, about a hundred yards from the church and meetinghouse.

"What if he's got a gun or something?" Russell said.

"He can't shoot us all," I said.

"He can if we all go in," Russell said.

"I'll go in," I said.

"And me," Joanie said.

Everyone looked at her. And at me. You couldn't expect a girl to go in. But she wanted to. She'd snuck in upstairs at Miss Delaney's house with me. The truth was, I felt safer with her along. I didn't know why. She couldn't do anything if Tupper did have a gun.

"Okay," I said. "Me and Joanie will go in. The rest of you will string out along the road. Russell will be right at the turn where he can see and hear what's going on. Then down the road farther, but where he can still see Russell, will be Nick, and farther down will be Manny and farther will be Billy. Anything happens, you can signal each other and take off for the cops. . . . You all know where the police station is in Searsville?"

They all did.

"Anything happens . . . any gunshots . . . or you get a signal from me or Joanie or Russell, you know. All of you ride like hell for the station. Don't wait for me, or Joanie, or each other. All of you ride for the cops, whoever gets there first . . ."

They took their positions.

Joanie and I went on around the bend and into the gravel yard. There were no cars there. The door to the meetinghouse was half-open. We stood for a minute and listened. We didn't hear anything. We walked to the meetinghouse door.

"Stay outside," I said to Joanie, "so Russell can see you."

She nodded. Her face was pale and tight. Her eyes seemed even bigger than usual.

With a big clenched lump in the middle of my stomach, I pushed open the door and peeked in. Nothing. I went in. Nothing. No movement. No sound. I walked around the room. The folding chairs were stacked where we had stacked them before we had left on Sunday. The big flag with the cross on it was gone. I went back out.

"Nobody there," I said to Joanie.

She nodded. We walked to the church. She stayed out. I went in. Silence. Emptiness. Nothing. I went back out and shook my head. Both of us looked at the space where the shiny new trailer had been. It was gone. Joanie looked at me and smiled. I nodded.

"Gone," I said.

My knees felt a little shaky. So did my stomach.

"Gone with the wind," Joanie said.

She patted my shoulder.

"You did it, Bobby," she said. "You won."

I nodded. Then we got on our bikes and collected the rest of the Owls. Russell fell in with us as we passed him.

"Gone," I said.

Russell grinned and nodded.

Then Nick, then Manny, then Billy.

"Gone," I said each time. "Gone. Gone."

Together we formed a small close column, three rows of two. And rode to Edenville. In front of Miss Delaney's house we parked our bikes in a semicircle. I got off and walked to her door and rang the bell. In a moment I could hear her walking down the stairs.

She opened the door. Her face tightened up when she saw me, and past me to the other five on their bikes. "He's gone," I said.

She stepped out onto the little porch.

"Excuse me, Bobby?"

"Mr. Tupper is gone. We had a . . . a kind of meeting with him and told him if he didn't leave here and leave you alone, we'd tell the army where he was."

"Jesus, Mary, and Joseph," Miss Delaney said.

"He seemed kind of crazy about it," I said. "But there was six of us and he couldn't catch any of us, and . . . he's gone."

"You're sure?"

"Meeting hall's empty, church is empty, house trailer's gone, car is gone," I said. "He's gone."

She sat down all of a sudden on the front step, with her skirt tucked under her, and hugged her knees and began to rock a little.

"My God," she said. "Oh my God."

I didn't know what to do. I patted her shoulder and she put her hand up and placed it on mine and kept rocking and saying, "Oh my God."

Behind me, Joanie said, "Come on, Bobby."

I looked back. Joanie jerked her head at me. I nodded and slipped my hand out from under Miss Delaney's.

"We'll talk later, Miss Delaney, just remember everything's all right now."

She nodded and began to cry. I went back to my bike and all of us rode away.

Nobody said anything for a time until Russell broke the silence.

"Think we'll all get A's in English?" Russell said.

"Except you," I said.

"I'd get one anyway," Russell said.

"Now all we got to do is win the state tourney," Nick said.

"Piece of cake," I said.

JOANIE and I sat alone on the bandstand on the last day of August. It was Saturday, Labor Day weekend. School was to start next week. Ninth grade. Edenville had no high school. This would be our last year. Next year we'd go to Eastfield High School or away to prep school. It would be different again.

"The town is really proud of you, Bobby," Joanie said, "all the Owls."

"The state tournament," I said.

"Yes."

"Been better," I said, "if we won it all."

"You got to the final game," she said. "Five kids without even a coach."

"I know," I said. "We did pretty good."

"And they don't even know what you did for Miss Delaney," Joanie said.

"We all did that," I said.

"But you figured it out," she said. "And, just like the basketball, you were the leader."

"I don't know if I could have done it without you," I said.

We were quiet for a bit. The harbor was full of sails. There were several younger kids down on the wharf, fishing for scup and catching blowfish. Some of the older guys were parked on the edge of the wharf, sitting on the hoods of their cars, talking.

"It was great," I said, "wasn't it?"

"Yes."

"Even if nobody but us knows it," I said.

"Yes."

The weather was warm, but the breeze off the harbor made it nice where we were. A brown and white spaniel was searching the lawn in front of the bandstand. Tracking some popcorn, maybe, that people had spilled last night.

There was something about the view: the green lawn sloping down to the water, the sun shining, the nice breeze, the happy dog cruising around on the grass, it made me feel good. I guess I thought my life might be like that: sea breeze and sunshine and green grass . . . and Joanie.

"You think we might start dating when we get a little older?" I said.

"Maybe," she said.

My throat tightened up a little, but I said it.

"You think we might get married someday?"

"Maybe," Joanie said.

"But?"

"But I think sometimes, what if we get to be boyfriend and girlfriend," she said, "and husband and wife . . . will I lose my best friend?"

"No," I said. "You won't."

And she never did.